LETHAL INJECTION

JIM
LETHAL INJECTION
NISBET

OVERLOOK PRESS

New York

First published in paperback in the United States in 2010 by
The Overlook Press, Peter Mayer Publishers, Inc.

NEW YORK
141 Wooster Street
New York, NY 10012

Cataloging-in-Publication Data is available from the Library of Congress

Printed in the United States of America
FIRST EDITION
1 3 5 7 9 8 6 4 2
ISBN 978-1-59020-195-4

LETHAL INJECTION

· ONE ·

The priest had a cold in his nose and an uncertainty as to his sexual identity; he'd never performed this service before; and there was an optional line in the prayers he had to get right. The printer had clearly marked the line in the text by enclosing it in brackets and setting it in italics.

[*especially those who are condemned to die*]

O.K., he thought, here goes.

"O God, who sparest when we deserve punishment, and in thy wrath rememberest mercy ..." Here he nodded toward the prisoner, his deference separating the insignificance of his own priestly suffering from the enormity of the prisoner's crime, but including both within the magnanimity of the wrath and mercy matrix. "... we humbly beseech thee, of thy goodness, to comfort and succor all prisoners," here it is; he cleared his throat politely and said it, "especially those who are condemned to die."

The priest paused and blew his nose. He had read it correctly, the italicized insert in the *Prayer for Prisoners*. Though the phrase was clearly optional, he'd inadvertently included it in the prayer one sleepy Sunday morning, while reading it to an old con with a touch of malaria doing a mere one-to-five for passing bad checks. To put it mildly, the oversight had exacerbated the man's delirium.

"Especially," he repeated quietly, not without a touch of satisfaction, "those who are condemned to die." He mopped his brow and replaced the wadded and filthy Kleenex among the ballpoint pens and mechanical pencils stamped with the names of various funeral homes in the inner pocket of his black linen coat, and sniffled.

Wreathed in chains, shirtless, Bobby Mencken sweltered on the edge of his bunk as he strove to take in every detail of the proceedings. Not that these details weren't readily apparent to him—in fact, each minute facet of the cell asserted itself to him as never before; he felt veritably besieged by the infinitesimal. But the problem was not in his perception of these details nor in his ability to concentrate on them. The problem was that each detail vied for its individual importance, clamored for equality or superiority to all others, while most of his brain, or at least that part of his brain that he'd left in charge of such things howsoever many haywire events, details and years ago, refused to accept an iota of what was happening to him as significant, meaningful, or important. So much had happened to Bobby Mencken, so much had gone wrong....

Why worry now?

"Give them a right understanding of themselves, and of thy promises; that, trusting wholly in thy mercy, they may not place their confidence anywhere but in thee...."

Due to the priest's nasal congestion, "Mercy" came out as "merdzy." Bobby, who knew a little French, remonstrated or "high-fived" with his brain a moment on its unhesitating taste toward making the obvious pun, converting "merdzy" to "merde-y," but tacitly agreed with the image of a life passed in a haze of shit, before he drew its attention to the irony of the meaning of the full statement, "right understanding of themselves, and of thy promises." Bobby looked at his manacled wrists, and turned his hands palms upward, accompanied by a gentle clinking as the links of chain resettled. All his life he'd trusted these hands to get him out of whatever scrapes his mind had gotten him into. Warden Johanson had warned Bobby that he didn't like to let a man languish in chains as he waited to meet his Maker. But that was before Bobby had nearly choked to death a guard called Peters, nine months ago, with his bare hands. Therefore, guards had come in just before the priest arrived and manacled him. He passed his gaze over the shadowy figures lurking along the causeway outside his cell. There were now at least four of them there, in the combat boots and dark blue regulation jumpsuits with no pockets, belts or laces, specifically designed to keep unarmed guards overheated and mean while mingling with the "population." He knew them all. One was a former Green Beret; another wrestled Sumo on the weekends; a third made it a point of honor never to discuss his Masters Degree in Business Administration; and the fourth felt the same about his sadism. And—what's this, a fifth? Bobby cocked his head just a bit, to get a glance at the fifth guard, and his eyes hardened. It was Peters, who had the pointed, almost clipped ears, the ball-peened brain, the stubby legs, the tertiary syphilitic demeanor, the monaural instinct, the unquestioning eyes, the tenacity and the pinhead of his nickname, Pit Bull. Though Bobby had never heard the click of claws as Pit Bull Peters padded along the line, population consensus figured the man for having everything but the collar of his namesake, which, undoubtedly, lay on the floor of a hog-wire pen near Warden Johanson's office, attached by a short, thick chain to a well-anchored cement post. This particular bull, this guard Peters, was a killer, and everyone in the prison knew it; he'd killed five times in nine years without so much as a suspension without pay, and as a result was as renowned, as feared, as revered for his familiarity with sudden death as … as …

Pit Bull Peters was as renowned a killer as Bobby Mencken himself.

Bobby Mencken scowled and raked the sweat off his face with his forearm. He'd just as soon not have to think about Pit Bull Peters. Not tonight. Tonight, cool was going to be enough of a trick.

The priest, catching the prisoner's expression over the rims of the little square half-rim glasses perched on the tip of his sore, pink nose, frowned slightly.

"Relieve the distressed …," the priest recited, or rather, read, for he'd never been in a cell on Death Row, before or since Texas had re-instituted the death penalty. Anyway, he was clearly too disconcerted to rely on his memory, which was just as well, for the priest's words raised one of Bobby's eyebrows. No amount of Valium was going to relieve Bobby Mencken's distress, and he wondered how much they'd given him, but then, a further thought caused a rueful smile to crease his features. He'd been born black, athletic, pansexual, half-crazy, good-looking, loyal, irrational, fun-loving, smart, eager, terrified and broke.

Would even death end his "distress"?

"... protect the innocent, awaken the guilty ..."

The smile collapsed, and Bobby's breath quickened. It was true that Valium had a certain effect on the merit he attributed to the circumstances around him, but it didn't make him stupid. Like his last meal, the remains of which were piled on a tray next to him on the bunk, the priest had come with the program, and he didn't want to miss a thing. But no prayer for those hopelessly maligned by fate was going to alter that fate, God or no God, any more than the consumption of kiwi fruit, cantaloupe, honeydew melon, nine grain bread, greens and sprouts salad, and semolina pasta dressed in uncooked tomatoes, garlic, olive oil and fresh basil were going to improve his health over the next few days. He stared sightlessly at the priest's shoes and burped. The pungence of raw garlic assailed his nostrils. They'd probably had to go clear to Austin to get that kiwi fruit. He hoped so.

The priest hesitated in his recitation, sighed, and resumed.

Judging by the man's footwear, preaching wasn't bringing home any more bacon than robbing convenience stores might. A slight movement behind one of the priest's tattered black brogans caught Bobby's eye, and gradually the feelers, then the head, then the legs and flat thorax of a large brown cockroach appeared on the smooth stone floor between them.

"... and forasmuch as thou alone bringest light out of darkness, and good out of evil, grant to these..."

Bobby recognized the roach as a regular visitor to his cell; he could tell by the bright magenta nail polish striping its legs and back, which matched the scraped remains of color on his own fingernails. These, his nails, were grotesquely long, inasmuch as Johanson had rescinded most of Mencken's privileges, including possession of nail clippers or even access to a manicure, after the attack on Peters. Since Mencken made a point of never biting his nails, a habit he had come to consider a sign of weakness, his hands now resembled nothing so much as the claws of a vampire in some cheap horror movie: a movie too cheap, Mencken mused, to hire white vampires. He'd painted his nails and the roach's legs and back, one slow day, as he inhaled the fumes of the acetone thinner in the polish until the plastic bottle had gone dry with the pigment still in it. That had been at least eight months ago. The roach stood there in its six crimson stockings and striped fuselage, waving its feelers, as if conducting the rhythms of the prayer floating down from high above it, almost as if it were a performer on a stage, and the priest's black legs the surrounding curtains of a proscenium. Matilda the cockroach, little mistress of time and space, who could come and go in this place as she pleased, a testimonial to the ideal of effortless, stylish survival.

"... thy servants, that by the power of thy Holy Spirit they may be set free from the chains of sin ..."

Bobby shifted his gaze to the priest's face. The priest had put tremendous emphasis on the word "free"—set *free* from the *chains* of sin—as if speaking to a whole tent full of people. Aside from that, assholes like him had learned it from watching Martin Luther King on television. Could this fool really believe what he was reading? The priest was frail and pale and puffy, with thin sandy hair. His Adam's apple bobbed up and down his throat like a nervous commodities broker trading in mucus and obsequies. Thick black hairs curled over the slight knuckles of his finely boned hands, hands that had never known hard labor, hands that would blister as easily as the soft skin on the body would bruise. Bobby considered the praying minister, and his eyes assumed the cold look of appraisal peculiar to the hunter first sighting his quarry. What would it be like, he wondered, to have sex with this virginal priest? I could make him scream, he thought idly. But could I make him renounce his faith, mid-orgasm, just to gratuitously ruin him? He set about isolating himself within the delicate seams of a fleeting, fragile sexual fantasy. . . .

They both heard the steel clash of the electromechanical locks that segregated Death Row from the rest of the prison, and the first of a series of huge iron doors open, a long way down the causeway, nearly at the other end of the building. When the door closed and the long rods sealing it top and bottom shot home, their crashes coursed up and down the cell block, making everyone and everything they touched reverberate with the fear born of distant machinery in hell. No one could hear such sounds and not wonder what sad, ugly business they portended. The priest paused in his prayer, looked up, and found the prisoner already looking at him. Priest and prisoner exchanged glances, the former out of trepidation, pity, and respect for a man going so calmly to his death with a bellyful of health food—although, he was supposing, we can give wondrous comfort to a man such as this, with a little bit of prayer, not to mention a stiff dose of Valium. But as this thought flashed across his mind another interrupted it, which was, Prisoner Mencken, whom he'd never met before this midnight, was leering at him. Prisoner Mencken's face was a mask of pure lust, and in spite of the heat, the priest shivered. Lust was something he preferred to discuss through the grill of a confessional. He suddenly found himself out of his waters, so to speak, struck dumb and helpless, a frog watching a snake, doing nothing, waiting, sitting on the lily pad that was his faith, tonguing the fly that was his prayer, watching the glazed eyes in the blunt, triangular head of his fate.

But the crash of a second, closer door, and the sounds of several pairs of shoes striding slowly, purposefully down the ancient, worn stones of Huntsville, jolted the priest back to his duty, and he hastened to finish the Prayer for Prisoners Condemned to Die.

"... chains of, of sin ... and ... and may be brought to newness of life, through Jesus Christ our Lord. Amen. The almighty and merciful Lord grant thee pardon and remission of all thy sins, and the grace and comfort of the Holy Spirit bless you and keep you, all the days of your life. Amen." Whoops. He was rattled. Got the Absolution crossed with the Benediction. All the days of his life, indeed. The priest nodded his head, to cross himself anyway, and noticed the cockroach on the floor between his feet. A shudder ran through his delicate frame. If he'd been born Irish, he thought, he might be able to take this.

"A-fucking-men, Reverend," the prisoner rejoined, laughing. Though he hadn't darkened the door of a church in twenty years he knew a gaffe when he heard one. "All the days of my life, a-fucking-men. Come on, Matilda," he continued, apparently speaking to the roach, "join in with the congregation." He raised his voice at least an octave and repeated, "A-fucking-men, preacher man." Mencken laughed strangely, looked up at the priest, and shrugged. His chains rattled. "She's just another blasphemous entity, reverend, and knows no better." He paused. His smile faded. "Like me." He looked down at the roach and smiled. "She's come to say goodbye to me." He looked up at the priest. "Like You."

The priest, head bowed, his obeisant cruciform frozen in mid-gesture, looked up through his eyelashes, past his fingers touching the middle of his damp brow.

Prisoner Mencken opened his mouth slightly, raised his chin, and passed the tip of his tongue over the lower edges of his upper front teeth.

Though he had never witnessed so obscene a gesture, so pellucid a flirtation, from so close up, the priest demurely finished crossing himself, closed the prayer book around his forefinger, thus marking his place in the Last Rites, and took a step backward, all the while watching the floor. By the random shouts, taunts and curses emanating from the cells down the block, the two men could gauge the advance of the small party coming to guide the prisoner Mencken to the site of his final departure.

After a pause the priest stepped forward and crushed the cockroach beneath the sole of his shoe. The sound was not unlike that you would make if you were to suddenly clench your fist around an empty matchbox. He turned his shoe a little to the left, and a little to the right. Then, still looking downwards, the priest took a step back again.

Equidistant between them on the floor lay a brown and yellow pulp. Here and there in it thin magenta sticks hinted that this had once been a cockroach with its legs painted in red nail polish by Prisoner 61-204 in his cell on Death Row.

The priest, in his fumbling way, while mulling further silent entreaties to his God regarding His memory and the prisoner's soul, had absently thought to make a minor improvement in the last fleeting moments of the prisoner's squalid lot on earth. He may even have expected some gruff form of gratitude from the prisoner, along the lines of, "Heh, well Revern', I reckin dey gots 'em in hebben, too, 'cause, Lawd knows, dey's plenty of 'em on dis ert.'"

Mencken, on the contrary, looked at the smear on the floor and smelled the world around him, and saw its lurid colorlessness, which he knew all too well, and recognized that only one life in this cell remained to be snuffed out tonight. He had once tried the seaweed soup in a dingy basement Chinese restaurant in Oklahoma City, and what he'd been served had portended the odor, the taste, the color, and the consistency of life in this prison lo, these two years. The inedible soup had tasted of old tires, creosote, diesel fuel and fetid muck, of barnacled pilings rotting in the sun. For five years he'd wallowed in the stench, the monotones, the clanks and scrapes and groans, the thrice-breathed air, the purgatorial screams, the locker-room putrefaction of decomposing flesh, ruined bowels, and doomed souls passing month after month, year after year, decade after decade, rooted to a stone place that could offer no nourishment, in an atmosphere that provided no light, in a world that offered no hope. Yet he had waited, while forces larger than himself argued in an impenetrably arcane language over whether he should be allowed to die immediately, or languish and dwindle and gradually decompose in a small tiled room like this one over the next forty to sixty years. Waited for he knew not what, nor whom, nor how, nor when, steeling himself against prayer, miracle, magic, delusion, hallucination, metempsychosis— fortified only by pride, violence, vigilance, calisthenic regimen, an abiding hatred and … hope?

Mencken almost stopped breathing as he stared at the miserable remains of a miserable pet cockroach he'd named Matilda, and cursed his miserable self. Roger, check, ten-four, yes, hope, hopeless hope. He had permitted himself to nurture a pathetic seedling of hope that ran deep, hidden, and completely through his most inner self, and only that hope had allowed him to endure two years in this solitary room. Without that hope he'd never have laughed, slept, dreamed, or awakened in this infernal hive more than a night or two, let alone worked up the stupidity to strike a blow for decency by trying to kill Peters. But even then, hope had given him the sustenance and forbearance to endure the evil half-life of solitary imprisonment. And now?

Ever since his childhood, and now more than ever, he'd been able to sit so perfectly still that he could sense the vibratory edge of chaos on which everything balances, beyond which he might phase into a blur, amazed that the sheer power of his hatred couldn't merely disintegrate the world— or at least its walls—around him.

Death and freedom, each contrapositive to the other, had become opposite, equivalent and interchangeable in the other's syllogism: each the fulfillment of the other's hope.

Not only that, he failed to laugh, that soup had cost him two bucks.

He sat, perched on the edge of his rude bed, and looked at the shoes arriving beyond the bars of his cell door, waiting in the causeway. Was his executioner among them? Who, among these functionaries, was to put the needles in his arms, and flick the valves, to inject a cunning deadly fluid that would jet into his heart the terminal blackness, spreading like the ink of a squid shot into the sea around it?

His chains rattled as he covered the inside of his right elbow with the palm of his left hand and rubbed a scarred vein pulsing there. Though much abused in the past, his veins were now by the ironic virtue of two years of workouts in the prison gymnasium very thick and strong and prominent: healthy, as it were. It had been hope that caused him to pump iron on a daily basis, pushing himself to a previously unknown extreme of physical endeavor. He stretched out both his arms and looked at them. His triceps, biceps, pectorals, the forearms, all had grown shapely and powerful—quite the reversal for the scrawny junkie a mere two cops had bludgeoned a confession out of, in the back of a Dallas jailhouse, three and a half years before.

He flexed his arms, one then the other, and the tattoos running the lengths of both of them waxed and waned accordingly. Colleen… Would she make good use of this body now? It might show even Fast Eddie a lubricious thing or two. He touched the twin circular scars on his shoulder. Quickly, he dismissed these names from his mind. They were emotional substantives, fraught with feelings which for two years he had refused to allow himself to feel, ever since the final sentencing that would ultimately, all appeals having failed, send him to his death. Still... He flexed his arms again, the musculature swelled and rolled, rippling as he'd learned to make it do in front of the scratched and pitted plexi-encased gymnasium mirrors. Not bad, not bad. No punk in population had ever denied him, even a boyish guard or two had tumbled to the allure of this physique, perpetrator of pleasure, perpetrator of death.

Still, would they give him a choice? Which drug? And exactly which veins would receive the deadly point? And, what kind of point, what kind of dope? Dopes plural, it was rumored up and down the line. He half laughed, confident in the thought that the state would provide the finest drugs available to ensure his thorough demise. And in spite of the intense summer heat a shiver passed over him, and his naked flesh came up in goose bumps. An icy void swallowed his laugh and he hugged himself. The loop of chain connecting his wrists sagged against his chest. Its links felt warm on the cringing flesh.

Then they were all at the door. Warden Johanson, Pit Bull Peters, a man from the governor's office, the other four guards, various attendants. One of them keyed the lock.

Peters stepped into the cell, with an expression on his face that could only be described as thanatophagous—"death-eating." He stood a moment. The door slid closed behind him.

Whoa, thought Mencken, and sharp, paranoiac adrenalin chased the languid Valium from the operation centers of his metabolism. Without moving so much as a facial muscle to betray his redoubled perspicacity, every fiber of Mencken's body keened alert. The feeble incandescent light in the cell seemed to glow brighter with each insect that ticked against it. Something was up. Putting Peters in the same cell with Mencken was a deliberate provocation, much as... His eyes flicked to the praying priest.

Much as the slaying of a pet cockroach had been?

Peters stood at parade rest, his skilled hands clasped behind his back, uncertain as to whether the priest were finished with the churchly rituals, but in the main waiting for Prisoner Mencken to make a false step on the way to his hot shot. The guard's body had the evil geometry of an inverted pyramid.

Slowly drawing his feet up onto the edge of the bunk, Mencken rested his forearms on his knees in front of him, and regarded his nemesis, calculating the distance between them as he puzzled. The time-honored ritual of such places demanded absolute courtesy toward a man condemned to die. Didn't it?

The cell was small, less than ten feet across; Mencken knew its dimensions exactly.

Peters' eyes shifted toward the authorities conferring beyond the bars. Johanson would have left him little leeway. There were many witnesses.

Peters' gaze shifted back to Mencken. Since Peters had entered the cell Mencken had not entirely taken his eyes off him. Mencken did of course have a last request. The authorities that ran this institution didn't indulge their charges such niceties, and Mencken knew that, but, until the sniveling priest had stepped on Matilda, he'd thought Peters might be its object. Mencken shifted his gaze to the priest, who returned Mencken's glare with a frank look of pity. Mencken shifted his eyes to Matilda, the mucilaginous pulp on the floor between them, then back again fiercely. A puzzled expression flitted over the priest's mild, unlined face, then a hint of consciousness concerning the enormity of his thoughtless deed began to distort it. Mencken's telepathic glare intensified, until it might have iced the blood of the elves in Santa's workshop, let alone that of the fainthearted priest, who suddenly realized he might actually be in danger, that the prisoner Mencken looked about to explode. Although he assumed any precipitous act on the part of the prisoner would be profoundly futile, the man of God was beginning to feel himself decidedly unsafe from Mencken's manic stare when the little round mouth full of sharp teeth in Peters' face opened, and the tapering canine features in the head surrounding it pointed just a bit extra as Peters breathed his version of the penultimate question.

"Ready, nigger?"

The priest looked at Peters and gasped aloud. Then he returned his eyes to the prisoner and blurted, "God bless you, my son!" and crossed himself in terrified outrage. Doing this he dropped his prayer book, likely thereby, Mencken was thinking calmly, reprieving his own life. For the priest's sudden outburst of sympathy startled Peters, who, making his last mistake in Texas, took his eyes off the condemned man.

· TWO ·

In the death chamber, Franklin Royce glanced again at the clock on the wall, then checked it against his watch. Five minutes after midnight. They were late. Most unusual. Executions were never late. If they were late, it was because they'd been called off. But the reprieve should arrive via telephone, if it were granted at the last minute. He looked at the telephone mounted on the pea-green wall beyond the stainless steel gurney, and exchanged glances with the man posted there specifically to answer it. They both knew it hadn't rung. So something had gone wrong.

Royce tugged at his right ear with his left hand, an habitual gesture. This was no easy job, executing criminals, and it would be just a little more—well, not tolerable exactly—perhaps less nerve-wracking if it were to go off on time. But in any case, executing criminals was not an easy job, and not one you ordinarily expect a doctor to abet. But execution was not a simple matter any more, not even in Texas. Anyone could hang a man, and quite a few people could pull a lever that released cyanide gas into an airtight room. A fewer number could properly electrocute a human; that was a job frequently botched. The half-burned corpus still twitching, requiring another thirty-second jolt of fourteen hundred volts, the lights dim again in the prison library, et cetera. But hardly anyone outside the medical profession could be found qualified to measure a lethal dose of poison and neatly prepare a man for the injection of it. Moreover, the law requires that a doctor take the subsequent measurements necessary to certify that life has indeed ceased.

Once the Supreme Court had reinstated capital punishment, in 1976, humane treatment became the issue. No matter how heinous the crime, nor how guilty the perpetrator, the execution had to be accomplished with dignity. A hanged man could take as long as twenty minutes to choke to death; he might not even die at all, if the fall failed to snap his neck. Electrocution often failed to achieve an immediate effect, and the intervening failure was horrifying. Cyanide worked, but administering it as a gas took time, and, inasmuch as a cyanide execution left the state with a room full of poison gas with a possible corpse sitting in the middle of it, it produced awkward aftereffects, difficult to clean up.

So the system had devolved upon injecting a lethal substance directly into the condemned's bloodstream as the most efficient method of execution, and most satisfying all round, both to the condemned man and those who had to watch.

Ten minutes after twelve.

In his capacity as competent medical man, Royce once again checked his equipment. He hadn't set up all of the apparatus yet, which was fortunate, because by now one or another of the solutions might have coagulated in the shaft of a needle. Royce was a fairly methodical man, determined to ensure that his technique would never be as shaky as his hands could be. His stethoscope he wore, of course, with the earpieces around his neck and the diaphragm in his shirt pocket. On a small wheeled table next to the stainless steel gurney lay a length of amber rubber tubing, two serum bottles, a spool of white adhesive tape, two syringes, a bottle of isopropyl alcohol, scissors, a roll of gauze, a small box of cotton, and the Velcro cuff, round gauge, associated tubing, and rubber bulb of the sphygmomanometer, with which to measure the blood pressure. All this was on top of a folder containing Prisoner 61-204's medical history, soon to be completed.

From a tall wheeled IV stand were draped various tubes, clamps and hangers, and a one-liter bag of a saline solution. The tubes swarmed around a glass manifold, from which a further network of tubing led to the wall. Beyond the wall, out of sight of everybody else connected with this affair, three volunteers, paid two hundred dollars each, would simultaneously unclamp three plastic tubes when given a signal. One of the tubes would introduce the mortal chemicals into the saline solution and thence into the condemned man's bloodstream.

Royce gently squeezed the one-liter bag. Its fluid level rose and fell accordingly. This bag contained a plentiful supply of a nontoxic saline solution, used to get the apparatus circulating. The method of circulation relied on the condemned man's own blood pressure.

On the table was a brown serum bottle with a pink rubber cap containing three compounds. A powerful barbiturate called sodium thiopental, commonly used as an anaesthetic in surgery, too much of which induces rapid pulmonary collapse. The salt potassium chloride stops the heart. And Pavulon is a muscle relaxant, also used in surgery, to induce paralysis so the patient won't twitch inadvertantly under the surgeon's knife. Tonight, all three were to be introduced into 61-204's bloodstream in massive overdose.

Everything was there. On the floor behind the steel entry door lay the knackered pigskin Gladstone bag containing the standard supplies appurtenant to general medical practice. The bag had come down to Royce from his grandfather through his uncle. Both relatives had practiced medicine in Texas, his grandfather of necessity engaging in a great deal of veterinary medicine to make ends meet. There had been, in those days, much more livestock in Texas than humanity.

Twelve-fifteen.

Royce had known the great man only slightly; he remembered him as very tall and thin, with a very full head of white hair permanently creased by the ever-present short-brimmed black Stetson, and a similarly full and white handlebar mustache. Though his grandfather's stern demeanor had been very humorless, and he'd remained a rock-hard veteran of cattle wars, cholera epidemics, gunshot wounds, oil fires and gored rodeo cowboys, Royce could never forget his first impression of the imposing mustache's uncanny resemblance to the large pair of curvilinear steer horns inverted over the door of his father's barn. By proxy, Grandfather had forgiven this irreverence when young Franklin Royce graduated from the University of San Francisco—though without honors—and returned to Texas with his MD. Grandfather's instructions to Franklin's Uncle Addison concerning the ancient Gladstone bag confirmed this absolution.

Although, Royce thought ruefully, for the thousandth time, he'd never really gotten the story behind the bullet hole in the bag.

Because Royce's father Jesse had chosen a beautiful wife and a large, run-down ranch over the medical profession, Royce's father had never quite gotten along with Grandfather, who always had Sunday dinner with his other son, on a neat spread well kept by a caretaker Uncle Addison supported with his own lucrative city practice. If Royce and his father wanted to have Sunday dinner with Grandfather, they had to go to Uncle Addison's. Mother never went, and nobody ever asked about her. Even at the tender age of seven or eight, young Franklin could sense the tension among the three older men. Once they'd had a particularly quiet and tense Sunday dinner, through which his father had sulked over his iced tea and said very little. Leaving the older men to their détente, wandering through the big, cool house, young Royce had found the Gladstone bag behind the open door to the parlor. The carefully organized tools within—the stethoscope, the bottles of pills and serums, the little reflex hammer with its pink triangular head and chrome handle, the glass syringes with stainless steel annult on their plungers—these had fascinated him. Riding the twenty-three dusty miles home from Addison's place, Royce asked his father about the bullet hole. "Aw hell, Franklin," his father had flicked the reins over the back of the horse in front of them, "he probably had the goddamn bag with him at the goddamn Alamo."

Twenty after twelve.

The room in which the execution was scheduled to have taken place twenty minutes ago originally had been designed as a gas chamber. This design still served. The room was hexagonal. Its terra cotta tile floor sloped down slightly toward a central four-inch drain. Against one wall of the hexagon stood a large and sturdily built wooden chair, crisscrossed by thick leather straps with heavy metal buckles, each with two tongues. A small trap door was set into the wall beneath the chair, about a foot off the floor. At a signal from the warden, pellets of sodium cyanide were dropped through the door. These fell into a beaker of sulphuric acid beneath the chair, and the ensuing reaction released cyanide gas into the room. A complicated system of circulatory fans evenly spaced through the room, and its shape, were theoretically to ensure even distribution of the deadly fumes. But the condemned was securely strapped into the chair directly above and as close as possible to the origins of the fumes, to maximize the possibility of his choking to death sooner than later. The method almost always worked, but sometimes took a long time—particularly if the condemned man tried to hold his breath.

The wall directly across the room from the chair was glass waist-high to the ceiling and now had curtains drawn over it. Beyond were two rows of benches and room to stand, for the witnesses required by law. The window was double glazed, to ensure containment of the cyanide fumes, but because of the inadvertent soundproofing a microphone had to be installed in the death chamber, with a speaker in the wall over the witnesses, so that they could hear the condemned's last words, perhaps a blurted confession. No one ever came away from one of these events without remarking on the strange effect of watching the condemned man's death throes through the thick window while hearing him choke over a cheap sound system prone to distortion and squeals of feedback. Every journalist who had ever witnessed an execution here for the first time had gone away to write that no criminal, having spent a midnight among the witnesses on the other side of the glass from such an execution, would fail to mend his ways.

In modern times, the system was little changed. A stainless steel gurney had replaced the wooden chair, and the lethal injection had superseded the rope, the electrodes, and the cyanide pellets. But the window remained, as did the custom of admitting a certain number of witnesses, as did the direct line to the governor's office, as did the curious possibility of the last minute reprieve, as did capital punishment, as did capital crime.

At twenty-five minutes after the hour of midnight, just as Franklin Royce and the anonymous guard standing by the telephone had begun to run out of introspective thoughts, and were contemplating speaking to one another to pass the time, the door to the death chamber burst open. An excited guard in the blue jumpsuit and crepe-soled paratrooper boots worn by the men in his profession hurried in to address the only two men in the room.

"He's killed Peters!"

Royce and the man at the telephone stared uncomprehendingly.

"Who has?" said the man at the phone.

"Mencken! Killed him in a flash, just like that, broke his goddamn neck with the chain between his wrists when Peters went in to get him! Cleanest hit you ever saw," he snapped his fingers, "just like that. And his legs was still chained to his bunk!"

The guard at the telephone, who was black, allowed himself a grin and said, rather matter-of-factly, "Why that nigger so-and-so."

Although the twenty-minute walk from the front gate to the gas chamber, as it was still called here, could be most astonishing to the layman, even at midnight, Royce knew little of what went on in prison society. But from the black guard's expression it was easy to tell that this messenger would have to travel yet a little further before he found someone by whom this fellow Peters would be missed.

"I'll get my bag," Royce said.

"No need," said the messenger, "They've already hauled him to the infirmary. Warden says for you all to sit tight. They're going to put Mencken down anyway."

"Without a trial?" asked the man at the telephone.

"Already had one trial," said the messenger. "Warden says this man's been enough trouble already, and that Peters died in his line of duty, which at the time was escorting Mencken to his last reward. And to his last reward is where he's going to go. Tonight."

The man looked again at Royce. "Warden says to say they'll be right along. The prisoner's having a little trouble working up his nerve."

Little doubt about what that meant. The messenger disappeared the way he had come, leaving the door open.

"Now all we need," the man at the telephone said as if to himself, "is for this here phone to commence ringing."

Fresh sounds began to reach them from the hallway; of steel doors opening; of men blowing kisses, whistling, yelling goodbyes, insults and shouts; clanks, crashes, then silence; followed by the sounds of many crepe-soled footsteps, and something being dragged down the hallway. Out of the corner of his eye Royce saw the curtain secluding the witness room draw back, and he glanced toward it. Several men and two women stood uncertainly among the benches beyond the glass. One he recognized as columnist from the *Dallas Star*, a staunch defender of the death penalty. The others he imagined as members of the press and of the government, perhaps from the district attorney's office. He really had never wondered about the people who came to these things, why they came, who they were. But he wondered how long it would be before one or several of these people were joined or replaced by television cameras. Now he looked at them, and they at him. Once the curtains had been drawn back the fascination with death and its devices would not desert them, until the curtains had closed again. What did they think of him, the physician beyond the window, as he rolled the sleeves of his white shirt to his elbows, and removed his tie? Damp patches of sweat had appeared beneath the arms of his shirt and in the small of his back, but perspiration was never unusual in summertime Texas, even at night. He became aware of the hum of the long twin fluorescent tubes overhead, which ran exactly the length of the gurney. Because both the door to the gas chamber and the door to the witness room opened adjacent to each other onto the same hallway, he had just begun to discern the mutter of subdued conversation among the witnesses when the insistent muddle of rubber-shod feet eclipsed it, and five guards arrived at the door dragging the sagging shirtless form of Prisoner 61-204. They'd beaten him senseless.

Royce's jaw tightened at the sight, and he shot a hard glance at Warden Johanson and Reverend Thomas, who followed the pathetic apparition through the door.

"What's this," Royce said coldly, not taking his eyes off Johanson, "a lynching?"

Warden Johanson was a big man, and a hard one. He'd been in corrections for thirty-two years and Huntsville had been his baby for eight of them. Mencken had given him a great deal of trouble. Had Johanson even taken the time to look personally into his case he might have found a conviction a little less neat that almost anyone would like to see in a capital case, but a conviction, by a jury, it was, period. Johanson's job began afterward, and he looked the part. He weighed at least two hundred fifty pounds, had a bald head and a broken nose and stood over six-foot-three in expensive leather riding boots some trusty kept immaculately shined for him. He always wore dark glasses and a broad-brimmed Stetson except, apparently, at executions, and a concho belt with a silver buckle fashioned into a bull's head with silver horns and turquoise eyes.

Johanson looked ruefully at Bobby Mencken, who was draped, apparently unconscious, between two guards, one for each arm. Mencken was bleeding profusely from many cuts and abrasions all over his upper torso, and already his face had begun to swell. "That's one tough sonofabitch," Johanson said, rubbing the knuckles of his right hand. "He just killed a good man in cold blood." He looked around and raised his voice. "Peters was the only man I trusted to get Mencken out of that cell when his time came." He lowered his voice and regarded the unconscious man. "He broke Peters' neck with that damn twelve-inch chain there, between his wrists." Royce could see arcs of blood beneath the iron cuffs. Johanson gestured toward Mencken and shook his head. "Then he spit in the man's face and kneed him in the balls as he died." He shot a fierce glance toward the red telephone. The man guarding it wiped a smile off his face. "Even with a reprieve," Johanson snarled, "he wouldn't live long back in population. The other guards won't put up with a man's killed one of their own." He sucked thoughtfully on a skinned knuckle. "I thought we were going to have to shoot the sonofabitch to get him down here." Royce raised an eyebrow. It was hard to believe Mencken had been capable of such an outburst of energy. Royce had prescribed Mencken enough Valium to tranquilize ten out-of-work actresses.

"Let's clean him up," Royce said.

"You clean him up," Johanson retorted.

"Wait," Royce said to the guards, who had been about to lay

Mencken on the table. "Hold him up. Someone get me some towels, and hand me the bag behind the door."

The four guards looked at Johanson, who nodded. "Don't turn him loose," he cautioned, and left the room. Royce saw him enter the room beyond the double-glass wall, no doubt to apologize for his institution's tardiness, and perhaps to temper any future printed assessment of the spectacle. Royce would have expected Johanson to know a little bit more about journalists than that.

A guard showed up with some towels. Royce saturated one in hydrogen peroxide and set about mopping the blood off Mencken's lacerated black torso.

"This is going to sting," he said as he gently began, on the off-chance that Mencken was conscious.

"Sting me, motherfucker," the man said through swollen, split lips, though his eyes remained closed and his breathing shallow.

"Tough guy," Royce said. The peroxide foamed reddish brown as it sluiced the open wounds. Royce had never seen the like of the tattoos that completely covered Mencken's upper torso and disappeared below the elastic waist of his blood- and sweat-stained prison whites. Unlike the simpleminded iconography of the average white prisoner's tattoos—spiders, guns, knives, manatees, et cetera—the designs on Mencken were abstract and completely foreign to Royce, as was their method of application. They enwrapped the man's body in layered strings of raised welts, as if necklaces of small beads had been inserted just beneath the skin, and attained their pigmentation only from the resulting scarification. Together with the mottled crimson tint flaking off the two long fingernails that hadn't been snapped off in the fight, Mencken's appearance was exotic.

"Yeah," the Negro whispered, his eyes remaining closed, "now I'm," his voice faded out, "toughest...."

Royce dabbed the towel at the split lips. When they curled away from the sting he could see Mencken's front teeth had been cracked. He looked at the sweltering guards holding Mencken. They stared back. None of them had escaped unscathed.

"What'd you kill him for?"

Mencken inefficiently spit flecks of red saliva. "My pencil," he sputtered weakly, "Put some … lead my … pencil.…"

Royce stood up and stepped back. He had done what he could.

"Get these chains off him and put him on the table."

The four guards raised Mencken off his feet and laid him across the table, while a fifth arranged the eight seat belts and two Velcro cuffs intended to confine the condemned man. They had Mencken's legs strapped and Royce had turned his attention to his valise when he heard a mighty groan.

"Hold him!" a guard shouted. Royce looked up to behold the extraordinary sight of Mencken bench pressing two grown men. On either side of the table, the feet of each guard holding Mencken's arms twitched above the floor, gradually inching upwards as Mencken, who undoubtedly had sustained a couple of broken ribs in the melee in his cell, his face streaming perspiration, drew each of his clenched fists full of custodial groin toward the ceiling. The guard perched in agony on each fist rose screaming as if suddenly, inexplicably buoyant.

"Stop him! Stop the mother!" This the man holding the straps neatly effected by springing lightly up over the edge of the table and dropping heavily on Mencken's solar plexus, knees first. All the air was immediately expelled from Mencken's body in a scream, taking his strength with it, and the man on Mencken's chest slammed a fist into the side of the prisoner's head. The blows knocked Mencken out, and the guards easily finished with the straps, taking their time. Royce stood by, horrified and helpless.

The guards then departed, leaving Mencken firmly secured to the stainless steel gurney, staring at the ceiling, his chest heaving, his breath a shallow whistle in his throat. He was drenched in pink-tinged sweat.

Royce glanced at the window. The warden was still in the witness room, glad-handing the members of the press with his back to the glass. But almost all of them stood staring into the execution chamber, pencils lifeless over their notepads, awed by what they had just witnessed.

Royce took a small, rubber-capped serum bottle from his bag.

"Listen," he said quietly to Mencken, "can you hear me?"

Mencken said nothing, struggling for breath with closed eyes.

Royce glanced at the bottle in his hand, then looked over to the black guard still manning the telephone on the wall. This man composed his face into an inscrutable mask and looked away.

"Can you hear me?" he whispered again.

"Man," came Mencken's voice hoarsely between gasps, "I'm … ridiculously … alert. Did I miss anything? Am I dead?"

"No, but you're very hurt."

"Hey," Mencken grunted, "you must be some kinda … doctor … or something…." A drop of blood appeared at one corner of his mouth and trickled over his cheek.

Royce blotted it away. "You were prepped with Valium?"

"Must be why …," Mencken coughed, "why I feel so … so calm, so serene…." His eyes remained closed, his face was a ruin of pain.

Royce spoke quickly. "Listen, I'm supposed to give local injections of lidocaine, to numb your arms before I put the IVs in. I want to add morphine, which will numb a lot more than just your elbow. But you have to promise me it will be our little secret. O.K.? Will you go for that?"

"Man," said Mencken immediately, "does a bear shit in the woods?"

"O.K." Royce glanced up at the man next to the telephone, who stared straight ahead. His job was to listen for the phone.

Royce loaded a small syringe with seven milligrams of morphine sulphate. The needle squeaked when he removed it from the rubber cap of the serum bottle. He pointed the syringe upward and cleared the air from it by slightly depressing the plunger. A small jet of fluid glinted towards the ceiling.

Mencken had opened his eyes. "Don't waste that stuff on the ceiling, man."

He tied off Mencken's left arm with the surgical tubing. A fine vein rose immediately in the hollow of the prisoner's elbow, and he swabbed it with cotton. The smell of alcohol suddenly permeated the room.

"I was wondering which one it was going to be," Mencken whispered.

"Sorry," Royce replied softly, "I usually ask, but the left was convenient. Anyway, later it's both." When its point punctured the curved wall of the vein Royce deftly lowered the hypodermic and slid in the length of the needle. He pulled back a bit on the plunger, and a red plume blossomed through the transparent length of the syringe. Then he slowly pressed the plunger, forcing the contents of the syringe into Mencken's arm, and loosed the knot in the tubing.

"Ohhhh," Mencken breathed aloud, "Doctor …," and he lifted his pelvis as far as the straps allowed it above the surface of the table, toward the ceiling, and rotated it obscenely, if feebly.

Royce was appalled and astounded at the physical and spiritual defiance exhibited by this man strapped to the table, who faced death without allowing his contempt for everything around him to flag for so much as a moment.

"Hey, Doc." Mencken's voice was drowsy, relaxed.

"Yes?"

"Boot it?"

So this Mencken, if nothing else, was a junkie, or had been. Royce was familiar with the term. Mencken was asking him to pull some of Mencken's blood back into the syringe, then return it into his bloodstream, two or three times. Under the circumstances and logic of ordinary heroin addiction this practice assured the user of getting every last drop of precious dope out of the syringe. In any case, it was a psycho-sexual contrivance quite beneath the ethics of tonight's endeavor. "Trust me," Royce said, removing the needle.

Mencken relaxed and sighed shakily, deeply. "Man, that … feels good.…"

"Try not to nod out," Royce asked. "It'll look a little funny if you can't stay awake for … you know.…" Maybe I'll use smelling salts, Royce thought.

"Doc?"

"Yes, keep talking; that'll help."

"Doc, are you hip … to the irony … of your present … humanitarian … endeavor?"

Mencken's voice was powerless. Royce looked at him. The man's eyes were still clenched against the pain of the beating he had just suffered, and his bloodstream was coursing with morphine, yet he was as alert as anyone might be expected to be, on the threshold of his own execution.

"You mean, easing your pain somewhat, making you as comfortable as possible, just before they kill you?"

"Ye … Yeah.…"

"More or less, Mencken. More or less."

"Yeah," Mencken smiled distantly, "me too. We … could have an interesting … discussion.…"

"I talk to myself about it all the time," Royce muttered. He pressed a cotton swab soaked in alcohol over the bead of blood that appeared in the mouth of the tiny wound, whence he'd removed the needle.

"Doc," Mencken whispered.

"Yes, Mencken?"

Mencken made slits of his eyes and looked at Royce. His voice came and went but his gaze was constant. "It's more ironic … than you … think.…"

Royce held the wet brown shrinking eyes a moment with his own, then looked away. "I'm sure it is, Mencken," he said. "I'm sure it is."

"Yeah.… More.…" Mencken sighed and closed his eyes again.

Royce busied himself attending the details of the procedure. He quickly introduced a small amount of lidocaine, a local anesthetic, intramuscularly into each of Mencken's forearms, just below the inside of the elbow. Again the room was very still and as he worked Royce could hear Johanson drawling officially in the other room. He was fielding questions from the press.

After a moment Royce tapped the first arm he'd injected.

"Feel that?"

Mencken said nothing.

"Speak up," Royce coaxed him. "The IVs are pretty uncomfortable."

"Don't feel it," Mencken whispered, then cleared his throat.

"O.K." Royce uncoiled a tube from the stainless steel rack against the wall and fitted a sterile sixteen gauge needle to it. He checked the length of tubing for bubbles of air, then released a clamp on the tube until gravity forced a drop of fluid to appear in the hollow oval at the needle's tip. Then he reclamped it.

"Here's the first one," he said quietly. "You'll feel some pressure." He pressed the thick needle into the vein. Mencken forced a little air through his nose, but his eyes remained slits and he said nothing.

Royce wrapped a band of white tape around the tube and sweat-dampened forearm. He repeated the process at the other arm, then released the clamps on the two tubes. Soon a red loop of blood and saline solution began to circulate from Mencken's left arm, through the network of tubes and the glass manifold, and back into his right arm.

As Royce watched this plumbing he exchanged glances with the man standing watch over the telephone. As a prison guard this individual had probably seen everything twice, but the preparation for the injection was a hard thing for him to watch. Now he puffed out his cheeks, exhaling slowly, and pressed a handkerchief to his brow as he looked away.

Royce touched the condemned man's shoulder. "All set."

Mencken stared at the ceiling. "Jambalaya," he said.

· THREE ·

Having blown his nose and donned his chasuble, the priest entered the death chamber followed by Warden Johanson. Each had a part to play, and forgetting the recent violence so closely witnessed by both, each began to play it.

"Almighty God," the priest sighed, "with whom do live the spirits of just men made perfect, after they are delivered from their earthly prisons; we humbly commend the soul of this thy servant, out dear brother, into thy hands, as into the hands of a faithful Creator, and most merciful Saviour; beseeching thee, that it may be precious in thy sight . . ."

And onward. While the priest was reading, a guard slammed the steel door to the entrance of the gas chamber with hardly any finesse at all. The clock on the wall read a quarter to one. Things took on a certain inevitability. Beads of sweat gleamed densely on Mencken's upturned face. Johanson rocked back and forth off the toes and heels of his riding boots and clasped and unclasped his hands behind his back. The guard standing by the telephone stifled a yawn.

"Warden," Royce said, just as the priest standing next to the supine prisoner began another prayer.

"Dr. Royce?"

Royce indicated the twelve-inch white clock with a sweep second hand high on the wall above the telephone. "Has it occurred to you that there's no chance of reprieve now? Look at the time."

Johanson didn't look at the clock. "What about it?"

"The governor's staff thinks this man has been dead for forty-five minutes. Shouldn't you call and tell them there's been a delay?"

Johanson glowered. "You do your job and I'll look after mine, Dr. Royce." He gestured toward Mencken. "This man's condemned to die, and he's going to die. We're running late."

Johanson turned toward the priest and barked, "You finished?"

The priest, his head bowed in prayer, looked up.

"Good," said Johanson. He unfolded a typewritten page from his hip pocket and read it aloud.

"Robert Lambert Mencken, by order of the Superior Court of the State of Texas, having been tried and convicted of the capital crime of murder in the first degree, and having exhausted all manner of pleas and appeals thereof; and condemned to die by that court, no subsequent judicial review having found fault with that judgement; you are at this hour to fulfill the order of that court, whose sentence upon you is that of death, to be accomplished by the introduction of lethal chemicals into your bloodstream, until such time as all life shall have ceased to inhabit your earthly body. As deemed humane and required by the State of Texas, statute number 2838-21.5 ratified by the Supreme Court of the United States of America, in the year of our Lord nineteen hundred and seventy-six, and not subsequently rescinded."

Warden Johanson paused to pass a gray handkerchief over his brow. Silence reigned in the room. Beyond the doubleglazed window six witnesses sat in the double row of benches, and a seventh stood to one side. Except that a few were making notes, they might have been watching television.

"In accordance with this statute, Robert Lambert Mencken, you have received the final meal of your choice, and retained the possibility of intervention from the clemency and mercy of the State, as represented by the sovereign governor of this State, until the last possible moment. As warden of this prison and agent of that State, I now inform you that, all possibility of appeal, reprieve and clemency being exhausted, the will of the people of Texas will now be carried out. May God have mercy on your soul."

Johanson folded the paper, replaced it in his hip pocket and looked at Royce.

"Dr. Royce, it is understood that as a member of medical profession, you are here solely in your humane capacity, to ensure that the condemned man suffers as little as possible during the course of his punishment, to see it administered with compassion; and that you are not here to actually administer this lethal potion to him. This being understood, are you prepared to ready the prisoner for the injection?"

"I am," said Royce.

"Robert Lambert Mencken," continued Johanson, "do you have any last words?"

When Mencken failed to respond to this question, Royce thought he might have been overwhelmed by the morphine. Mencken's eyes were closed; his breathing was quiet; he looked very comfortable. Royce thought of the bottle of smelling salts in his bag.

Johanson addressed the witnesses. "The condemned Robert Lambert Mencken has nothing to say for himself. If Doctor Royce—"

"How about, 'I'm glad I killed him'?" said Mencken in a strong, clear voice.

Johanson turned.

Silence.

Johanson and Royce exchanged a glance.

Johanson's face suddenly went purplish red. Royce could see where he'd scoured his jowls with a safety razor at five-thirty every morning for forty-five years. Johanson was suddenly shouting. "And what about that poor mother of five you blew away for a six-pack!"

Mencken's eyes snapped open, flooded with pain. His face twisted with outrage. "I didn't—" He stopped.

"You didn't," Johanson snarled, his voice dripping with contempt.

But Mencken was watching Royce. Royce watched Mencken's eyes. The face relaxed, but the eyes reiterated the plea. *"I didn't,"* they said, as eloquently as the man's voice—perhaps more so. But Mencken's mouth jerked into a sneer and he said, "I didn't mean to kill Pit Bull, Warden. I was just trying to paralyze the sonofabitch for life." He closed his eyes.

"Peters was a God-fearing man doing his duty as he saw—"

Johanson stopped midsentence. His mouth contorted his face into an ugly mask and a muscle twitched in his cheek. A moment, then two passed.

"Is that all the prisoner wished to say?" Johanson said in an official, dispassionate voice.

Silence.

"Dr. Royce." Johanson turned and took up a position against the wall, next to the red telephone that connected the gas chamber to the office of the governor of Texas.

Royce looked at the telephone. Since midnight there had been no chance of its ringing. Before midnight there had been damn little chance. It was Friday night, or rather, Saturday morning. It was very likely that the governor hadn't yet sent home the last guests from a large fund-raising barbecue on his ranch, two hundred miles from the governor's mansion in Austin.

Royce approached the small table to the right of the strapped prisoner and took up the Velcro cuff of the sphygmomanometer. As he wrapped it around Mencken's left bicep, Mencken opened his eyes.

"You allowed to talk?"

Royce looked at Johanson. Johanson said nothing.

Considering his position was roughly equivalent to that of a man standing in the door of an airplane without a parachute, letting the slipstream feel him out, Mencken was calm. "What's the score?" he asked. He might have been talking about a ball game or a rental agreement.

Royce drew a breath, then explained it in a soft voice, as he adjusted the rasping Velcro cuff.

"Right now the mainlines into your arms are circulating a harmless saline solution. When the warden gives the signal, three people beyond the wall behind you there will unclip three hoses. All the hoses have the salt running through them, into your system, but one will come from that bottle there." Royce nodded at the bottle on the small table, past the prisoner's head. Mencken rolled his eyes over and considered it.

"Nobody knows which hose is hot," Mencken said.

"Right. First thing, you'll feel sleepy. When you do, try to take a couple of deep breaths."

"Sure," said Mencken. "Don't I get to count backwards from one hundred?"

Royce tugged at his ear. "You won't have time."

Mencken sucked on a tooth. His face gleamed with perspiration. "How about, will I have time to say, 'The cocksucker deserved it'?"

"It's kind of doubtful."

"Whew. That's some technology."

"You'd be better off taking a couple of deep breaths. It makes it even faster, and you might not regurgitate that meal the warden was talking about."

"I wouldn't mind giving it back to him." He raised his head. "Hey, Johanson."

"Mr. Mencken," Johanson said.

"Want to kiss me good-bye?"

Johanson said nothing.

"It's my last request."

Johanson scowled..

"Warden doesn't like me." Mencken laid his head down.

"Denying a man's last request." He looked at the bottles on the table next to him. Royce pumped the bulb of the sphygmomanometer. "Hey, Doc," Mencken said sheepishly, "what's in that stuff?"

One-fifty over ninety. The blood pressure of a perfectly healthy man on morphine and adrenalin about to die from an overdose of three other chemicals after getting tuned up by four prison guards. Royce wiped the sweat off Mencken's chest with the blood-soaked towel end and applied his stethoscope. He felt like an ass, making sure this man was alive. Mencken had a strong heart, too, though it was beating a little fast at a hundred. He must be a little excited.

"Huh, Doc, say," Mencken's voice boomed through the tubes of the stethoscope, "you got a name?"

"Franklin. Franklin Royce," he replied, replacing the business end of the scope in his shirt pocket.

"Dr. Royce," Mencken smiled, "anyone ever called you Rolls?

Rolls Royce?" Mencken laughed, looked toward the warden, laughed again, then looked back. "Huh?"

Royce smiled slightly and shook his head. "You're the first."

But Mencken hadn't been waiting for an answer to his bad pun. "Wish somebody'd call, yeah. Don't nobody call me anymore." He laughed a short laugh and looked from Royce to the red telephone. "Hey man," he said to the patient guard next to the phone, "why don't you call Time or something, make sure that thing works? Warden there mighta snuck down here in the middle of the night and un-plugged it."

The guard stared straight ahead, standing at parade rest, hands behind his back, and licked his lips.

"You ever heard that phone ring when there was Blood on this table? Does that suggest anything to you, man? Huh?"

No one spoke.

"For that matter," Mencken's eyes searched the faces around him, "for that matter, has there ever been anybody other than Blood on this table? Huh?"

Royce fitted the tip of a large needle to the rubber cap of the bottle of poison and drove it through the seal.

Mencken turned his head, the only part of his body that he could still move against the restraining straps that bound him to the gurney, to watch Royce. Royce inverted the little bottle and held it to the light. Everyone in the room and beyond the glass watched, fascinated, as the tube below the needle slowly filled with a clear fluid. The deadly serum flowed slowly because it was thick, which was also why the needle used to inject it had to be a large one.

"Rolls Royce," Mencken breathed, watching him, "what's in that stuff?"

"Poison," Royce said.

"That's a relief," Mencken said absently, "I wouldn't want to be going through all this for nothing." He smiled. "Is it, you know, any good?"

"The best."

"Good as that other?"

Royce didn't think Johanson would appreciate that he'd given the prisoner some small relief in his last hour. He kept his eye on the fluid level in the bottle as he said quietly, "You tell me, Mr. Mencken."

Mencken snorted. "Yeah," he said, "I'll be beaming you superlatives from the astral envelope." He stared at the little bottle and the hose that hovered between him and the bright lights above.

Royce hung the bottle upside down on the IV rack, and let the hose that connected it to the wall dangle below.

Royce looked over Mencken at Johanson. Johanson frowned, and made a little circular movement with his hand and index finger, as if to say, "Get on with it." Royce moved to Mencken's side and looked down at him.

"Ready?"

Mencken briefly frowned, then suddenly scowled. He focused his eyes on Royce's face and said, "Ready? Ready? What does that mean, 'ready'? Ready for what? You mean am I ready to go to sleep now, like a good little boy—and I use the word 'boy' advisedly—and wake up in an hour in the same goddamn world, in the same goddamn room, on the same goddamn table, and have the white folks say, 'That's a good boy, Bobby, 'cause, since you didn't die, you must be Superman, and so this has all been a joke. Since you is survived the Bardos of chemical death, we agree with you, boy, it's all been a joke and you must be innocent, and now—are you ready for this? —you is free to go, you is a free man in a free society.'

"Yeah," Mencken said bitterly, "I'm ready for that."

Royce couldn't look Mencken in the eye.

"Don't look away from me, Doctor Royce, 'cause you're the only man I can see in this room, and the last thing I'm going to look at on this bleak earth. And that thought makes me happy, Doctor, because, hey, you want to know why I'm *ready*? I'm *ready* to get off this planet because as long as I can remember, it's been a very confusing, difficult place. You know why?

Royce fiddled with his stethoscope. "Why?"

"Because I'm tired of fighting a world that condemned me the day I was born, that's why. You think I'm jiving?"

Royce suddenly, inexplicably, caught the smell of the con-demned man full in the nostrils for the first time: blood, sweat, fear, garlic—Death.

Johanson cleared his throat. "Dr. Royce—"

"Think about it," Mencken shouted, his eyes going from Johanson to Royce's face. "I'm getting put down for the wrong thing here to-night, Doc, but I'm so used to it, I'm so *ready* for the flip-flop that *I'm not surprised,* Doc. You got that? This is nothing new, here. This has been happening to me all my life and I'm telling you that I have never, *ever!* suffered for the right reason! You hear me? *Never!* But I turned the tables on 'em tonight, yes I did. Tonight, at least, at the last pos-sible moment, I arranged to be going down for the right goddamn reason. Yes I did. Oh goody, oh boy, oh shit!"

Mencken's head fell back into a pool of perspiration tinged with blood on the surface of the stainless steel table, with a hollow, metal-lic thump, his teeth clenched in frustration. He was breathing hard. Tears filled his eyes.

"Fuck, I need a vacation," he said.

Royce hadn't notice the pool before. He folded a towel and gen-tly placed it beneath the black man's head.

Royce swallowed and looked at Johanson. This business was be-ginning to unnerve everybody; there was no sense in prolonging it. "Everything's set," he said. Neither Mencken nor Royce had noticed the priest, who had drawn near to be handy in case Mencken needed him.

Johanson didn't hesitate. He crossed between the telephone and the stainless steel table and banged his meaty fist on the wall three times.

Mencken jumped in his straps. The priest jumped in his cassock. Even Royce, who was watching Johanson, started at the first blow.

Johanson's face betrayed none of his pleasure as he resumed his position.

Royce placed his hand on Mencken's shoulder and watched the fluid level in the inverted bottle. After a moment, it began to drop. He waited. Mencken's skin was hot beneath his palm. A rope of muscle pooled at the point of the bone there. For the first time Royce noticed the small twin circles of scar tissue on the neck at his fingertips. Then he whispered, "A couple of deep breaths, now." By this time Royce was perspiring as heavily as Mencken, and the shoulder was slippery to his touch. The bottle was half-empty. Royce forced his eyes away from the bottle to look at Mencken.

The convict's eyes met Royce's, very large and dark and moist. Then Mencken yawned; it was the only sound in the room. Twice he inhaled deeply, each time as if he were having trouble getting his breath. His nostrils flared. He exhaled the second breath and held Royce's stare with his own. He shook his head, moving his lips.

Royce bent quickly to catch Mencken's last words.

"Colleen, I … didn't …," he whispered.

And he kissed Royce on the lips.

Royce quickly stood up astonished, touching his mouth. Mencken was still staring at him, but his eyes were sightless.

The slightest trace of a smile lingered about his lips.

· FOUR ·

The Texas night, immense, black, hot, flowed imperceptibly above the pickup, as effortlessly as the pickup flowed through a constant stream of moths, bugs and crushed armadillos. The Texas highway stretched straight and seemingly endless before and behind, its way infrequently traced by headlights in one direction and taillights in the other, with great, immeasurable distances between them. It was four-thirty in the morning and Royce had both windows down, and he was still sweating; but after the stifling claustrophobia of Huntsville the hot bluster at the cab windows felt like cool alpine breezes. He'd been driving southeast for almost an hour. One hand held the wheel, his elbow propped in the open window beside him. The other hand fidgeted with the cap of a bottle of whiskey he'd stopped to buy a half-hour after he'd passed through the last checkpoint at the prison perimeter, well beyond the actual walls.

Royce drove with the distracted attentiveness which is the particular preserve of Westerners, who often must drive a hundred miles or more to go to church, or to the sale barn or cattle auction, or to visit a relative for Sunday dinner. A hundred or so miles in a V-8 pickup truck, with a bull in the back, at seventy-five or eighty miles per hour, a man can get a funny look on his face. Under these conditions he can think over his whole life. He can go over the ranch books transaction by transaction, debit by credit, if he knows them well enough, or he can spend a whole hour mulling the single fact that he really doesn't know very much at all about bookkeeping. Or he can discern subtleties in the genealogies of cattle breeding that might have eluded him in less tranquil circumstances. Over the course of an hour his expression might not change much, but his mind will change, then go back to its original position, then change again to an entirely different, third opinion, then forget the whole thing.

If he has a phone in the truck, he can call his wife and ask her what she thinks about it, or somebody can call him and give their opinion.

The expense and network locations aside, a lot of folks don't have phones in their trucks for just that reason.

Franklin Royce had a great deal on his mind when he left Huntsville prison that night. Warden Johanson hadn't been much help.

"Y'ain't got the stomach for the job, y'best quit," he'd said.

Royce had the stomach for the job. It wasn't the job that was bothering him.

A half-hour out of Huntsville, he'd stopped by a road-house to buy a couple of beers.

It was the usual kind of joint: neon sign for Lone Star beer high in a cloud of bugs out front, with a half-dozen pickups parked in the dust around it. Some trucks with two bales of hay and a saddle in the bed, or maybe a couple of fifty-five-gallon drums of diesel, with a deer rifle or spinning rod slung on the gun rack in the cab, horse trailers hitched to two or three of them, each with a dozing horse or two or empty, as the big trucks sang by on the highway.

Inside was dark and cool, with a jukebox playing a Bob Wills tune. A game of Space Invaders played with itself in the back. Two men and a woman sat at the bar. The light of a television behind it played over their faces.

"Get a drink?" Royce asked a cowboy smoking at the bar.

"Might," the man said, not taking his eyes off the screen. The woman a couple of stools down the bar laid her cigarette in an ashtray and stood up slowly.

"What's it for ya?" she asked, as she circled the far end of the bar and walked up the duckboards behind it.

Royce sat at the bar and looked up at the television over his head. They were watching a news program. A tanned young man with perfectly coiffed white hair and a stack of papers in front of him spoke authoritatively into the camera.

"Two cans of Pearl in a sack," Royce said, "cold."

" 'At's a good beer," drawled the second man down the counter. As he spoke, a large picture of Bobby Mencken appeared on the screen behind the news commentator. It startled Royce.

"Specially when it's cold," the man down the bar continued, exhaling a cloud of smoke, "so's y'can't taste it." He pursed his lips and loudly spit a flake of tobacco off his tongue.

"Can you hear this?" Royce asked the man between them.

"Same shit every night," the man said, not taking his eyes off the screen. "Turn it up."

Royce stood on the rungs of his barstool and found the volume knob.

"... tonight at midnight. Mencken was convicted in 1983 of shooting a convenience store operator five times in the face for nine dollars during a robbery in the Dallas–Fort Worth area in 1982." The commentator spoke in the neutral, emphatic monotone taught him by a New York school of broadcasting, and sounded quite foreign in this Texas bar. "Mencken," he continued, "was apprehended fleeing the scene of the crime, moments after it was committed. He spent the next nine months in jail, while the district attorney's office built a case against him. Even though the prosecution provided no hard evidence and called no eyewitnesses to testify, Mencken was convicted of first degree murder with special circumstances. The entire case was based on the facts that police had apprehended Mencken fleeing the scene of the murder, and when the murder weapon was recovered the next day Mencken's fingerprints were on it."

"Uh-oh," somebody said.

"The jury deliberated less than two days. Because of the special circumstances, that the murder was committed in the course of an armed robbery, Judge Howard Lemur was able to hand down the maximum sentence prescribed by Texas law, death by lethal injection. The American Civil Liberties Union immediately filed appeals on Mencken's behalf. But the Superior Court upheld the conviction, and, late last month, the Supreme Court refused to hear the case." The commentator turned the top page of his stack of papers face down on his desk, as the picture of Mencken faded behind him. "Mencken was the seventh person," he added, "to face capital punishment in Texas since the United States Supreme Court reinstituted the death penalty in 1976." The camera angle changed. The commentator turned his face into it. "What are the Cowboys going to be up against in the fall? Sports in a moment."

"*Fuck* the Cowboys," said the man down the bar, rubbing his eyes with the heel of the hand that held his cigarette.

Royce reduced the volume and sat back on his barstool. No witnesses, the commentator had noted, but they sent Mencken over anyway.

"Damn," said the man next to Royce. "Shot the dude five times in the face?"

The woman behind the bar dropped two cans of beer into a brown paper bag in front of Royce. "Who says it was a dude?" she asked over her shoulder. "That'll be two-fifty," she said to Royce.

"It was? It was a woman? Hell, Ella, what kinda feller'd shoot a woman five times in the face?"

"That kind." She nodded at the television.

"But why? Why would he do it?"

"Maybe she was ugly," said the drunk next to him.

Everybody looked at him.

"Gawd amighty, George," the man next to Royce said, but he laughed anyway.

The woman behind the bar shook her head. "George," she said, "that's about enough outta you."

Royce looked at the bag containing the two beers. He brushed it aside with his forearm and neatly spread a ten-dollar bill on the bar. "Got any whiskey?" he asked.

"You're in Texas, ain'tcha?"

"Straight up."

She placed a shot glass on the counter and filled it. Royce raised it and toasted the second man down the bar. But he was really thinking of Mencken when he said, "Here's to humor in the face of the unknown."

"Goddamn," said the woman, "here's somebody knows something

about horses."

Royce downed the shot.

"Why would a man shoot anybody five times in the face?" the first man asked.

" 'Cause he didn't like him," George volunteered.

"Hm," nodded the first man. "Y'might have somethin' there, George."

"That's why *you* would shoot somebody five times in the face, George," the woman said.

"Nah," said George. "I'd jist use a shotgun an' be done with it."

"Maybe he just didn't want the woman to recognize him later," the first man said.

"Let alone recognize herself," George said.

"Now we're talkin'," the woman said. "The clerk runnin' the convenience store committed the robbery, and left behind some innocent heifer with her face blown off, so the cops couldn't tell it was the wrong heifer, and not the clerk. Only trick was gettin' that innocent jerk's fingerprints on the murder weapon, so then the clerk can accidentally lose it some place where the cops'll find it. At the Policeman's Ball, maybe. Jerk has a record so they know who he is. A year later he runs a stop sign, they run him through the traffic computer, bingo," she snapped her fingers, "he's on ice. Case solved. Meanwhile, the clerk's livin' it up in Brazil on the contents of the cash register." She looked at Royce. Royce looked at her. " 'Nother shot?"

Royce nodded.

"That's pretty good, Ella," George said.

"Hey," said Ella, pouring Royce a shot, "I grew up watchin' Perry Mason."

George frowned. "Y'mean your kids grew up watchin' Perry Mason."

"Stick to the current line a thought, George," Ella said sternly.

George opened his mouth, nodded and tapped the bar with a rigid forefinger. "There's just five or six hitches in it, which is about how many it takes to hold a mare fulla loco weed."

Ella lowered her voice. "What mare, George?"

George ignored her. "But one of the main ones is, ain't no convenience store clerk gettin' to no Brazil on no nine dollars, even if it is right next to Texas."

"I thought you were drunk, George," Ella said.

George shook his head. "Not that drunk."

"Have a belt." She placed a glass on the bar front of him. "On me."

"Obliged." George placed a couple of fingers delicately around the shot glass. The woman behind the bar filled it. George drank it all.

"Now go fall off your horse," Ella said.

"I think we were right the first time," the man nearer Royce said.

"What," Ella said, replacing the whiskey bottle beneath the counter, "he's drunk?"

"No, I think that colored feller on the television there killed that clerk because he didn't want to be recognized."

"They burned his ass anyway," George said.

"But," said the other man, "was it really him that did it?"

Royce, staring into the bottom of his empty shot glass, heard himself say, "Nobody else saw him."

The other man covered Royce's forearm with thick, calloused fingers. "That's right, hombre, nobody else saw him do it. It coulda been anybody."

"It mighta been you, Herb," George said.

"Yeah, yeah." Herb was excited.

"He said he was innocent," Royce muttered.

Herb frowned. "He did?"

"Not exactly. He said 'I didn't,' and he meant it. 'I didn't,'" Royce repeated absently. "But something stopped him."

"Where'd he say that?"

Royce looked up.

"Why—can't you see?" George interrupted, "can't you see? This feller was there, right there, when they shot that guy fulla dope in Huntsville. Deathbed confession, it was. This feller here was right there an' he heard every word of it, too." George smiled. "Didn't ya, young feller?"

All three eyed him curiously.

Royce looked down at his glass again and cleared his throat. "Oh, I—saw it in the paper, while back. I kinda followed the trial, you know, in the papers. Couple years ago," he added lamely.

"It's all right," Ella said in a consoling tone, patting Royce's arm. "Some of us can read; some of us can't."

"Yeah," Herb agreed doubtfully, looking up at the television flickering silently above Royce's head. "Even so, seems like they wouldn't come down that hard on a man, without they had some kinda hard evidence."

"That's true," George said. "I thought they hadda have at least two eyewitnesses before they'd give a man the death penalty."

"God forbid it should be the two a you," Ella said. "Couldn't tell a bull from a steer if it tried to mount you."

George squinted at Ella and passed one hand over the three or four days' of gray beard on his weathered face. "If it *was* ta mount one a us," George said, "it was 'cause you was the only other see-lection in the pasture."

"Why you cottonmouth sonofa—"

"Give us another round, Ella," Herb said, loudly and quickly. "One for yourself and the young feller here, too."

"I'm not—" Royce began.

"I'm not young either," Herb hastened to interrupt. "I'm completely over the hill. Let's have them, Ella. George is buyin'." Herb deftly slid George's change toward Ella.

George didn't move. "Hey," he said.

"Why, thanks," Ella smiled acidly, snatching the bills. "That's a mighty fine apology. Ya fuckin' old coot."

George shook his head, flapped his hand ineffectually, and said nothing.

Ella poured four whiskeys, then held her glass aloft. "To George," she said. "Never a finer cowpoke poked a cow."

George raised his glass and shook his head. "To the innocent man," he countered.

Lost in thought, Royce looked up and stared at George. George gestured at Royce with his glass. "The innocent man, mister, wherever he is."

This word innocent had its effect on Royce. It should have come up a lot earlier tonight, but it hadn't. The confidence that had allowed him to go to work tonight was deeply shaken. He had tried and failed to dismiss the evening's deeds as the machinations of Justice and the State, and of himself as just a cog in them. But a gnawing uncertainty was working on undermining and eroding his confidence in that process. And now, at the tail end of a silly conversation, he was being asked to superciliously toast the very specter of his uncertainty.

So he did. "To the innocent," he said. Then he added, "And the guilty, whoever we are. May we find our respective sinecures in hell." He tossed off his whiskey and set the glass, a little too loudly, down on the bar.

No one else drank to his toast, but sat or stood, their drinks raised, and looked at him. Royce ignored them. "Bartender," he said.

Ella raised an eyebrow.

"Could I trade you back these two Pearl beers, as a down payment on a bottle of Ezra Brooks?"

Ella shrugged and carefully placed her shot, untouched, beneath the bar. "That's tradin' up," she observed, taking the paper sack.

"Sonofabitch, hombre," George said suspiciously. "That was one mean *amor y pesetas* you put on us poor sinners, there."

Royce eyed him. "You a churchgoer?"

"Hah!" Herb slapped the bar.

George squinted one eye. "If I get your drift, mister, you think we're all goin' ta hell one way or another, no matter who we are or what we done."

"Naw, George," Herb put in, ever the one, apparently, to defuse a situation. "I'm sure he thinks it's just one big barrel a happy horse apples, just like you do."

"Shee-it," George growled softly, without unsquinting his glare at Royce.

Royce narrowed his eyes and wondered if George was right. The light in the bar was beginning to take on a yellowish quality.

Ella came back up the boards with a tall sack wrapped around a bottle. "Seventeen bucks," she said, placing the package on the counter, and added, "No tax for a man who can discuss higher concepts."

Royce added a ten to the ten already on the bar and left.

After the screen door had clapped shut and Royce's truck had gotten onto the highway, Herb raised his glass and said, "To the innocent."

The other two drank with him.

· FIVE ·

By the time he arrived home at a few minutes after four, Franklin Royce was a confused man. So confused that he snuck up on his wife's Mercedes in the driveway and allowed the pickup's high front bumper to quietly crush a rear taillight lens, which betrayed what he really thought of that car of hers. He had resented paying for it, not because a Mercedes was what she wanted, but because he couldn't afford it. But she said a doctor's wife should have a Mercedes, simple as that. Never mind that they'd had to drive five hundred miles to find it. Never mind that every time a tumbleweed rolled up under it the thing would catch on fire. Never mind that a tune-up cost almost a thousand dollars and—

For that matter, never mind that a new taillight lens would cost a hundred and sixteen dollars. That's right. One hundred sixteen dollars, *plus* installation.

After all, it was a Mercedes. Pamela's Mercedes.

Goddamn right, Pamela's Mercedes. He cut the wheel, backed up, cut the wheel the other way, drove forward. The other taillight trickled to the asphalt.

Two hundred thirty-two dollars. Plus installation.

He stepped out of the pickup with the bottle of whiskey and slammed the door. After a couple of steps he stopped, turned around, opened the door of the pickup and stashed the bottle behind the seat. There was still quite a bit of whiskey left in it, judging by its weight, and he could always use a bottle in the truck. Medical reasons. Sheee-it, he slammed the door. He turned 360 degrees and opened it again. He found the old Gladstone bag on the floorboard and pulled it out. Then he turned toward the house, but something kept him from moving.

All the lights were out. Pamela had long since finished watching Johnny Carson and gone to sleep. She could have left the porch light on for him.

That'll be the day.

It was always like this, now. Coming home had long since been bad. But lately the actual idea of going home stuck in his craw like a fishbone.

He heard crickets all around him, and particularly one loud one, which must have been in the weeds in front of him, next to the little sidewalk that led from the driveway to the house. The little sucker was really going at it. He remembered that the frequency of a cricket's whirring was supposed to correspond directly to its ambient temperature. The hotter the temperature around it, the faster the cricket whirred. If it gets hot enough, the crickets explode. That's why there's no crickets in Saudi Arabia. Yarggh.

He suddenly became aware of the immense Texas night. He leaned back and saw the millions upon millions of stars above him and almost fell over. He swayed and took a step forward. The cricket next to the walk stopped whirring abruptly. He took a step backward. Apparently the cricket was not to be fooled so easily. He backed up to the truck. Still no sound.

"All right," Royce said aloud. He placed the Gladstone bag in the bed of the truck and opened the door. He retrieved the fifth of whiskey and screwed off the cap.

"I got time," he said softly, and took a drink. It was good whiskey, very smooth. Made for sipping, they said, and in fact he hadn't had very much. But there was a lot more than whiskey tampering with his equilibrium, more than whiskey and Pamela, even.

Again he looked at the sky. There were a lot of stars up there.

A lot of people down here.

One less, tonight.

As he watched the stars he became aware that one of them was moving. A shooting star? The tiny light cut a straight, rapid path through all the others around it. A satellite. Man-made. He watched it go until it disappeared beyond the nebulous aura of light above

Houston, far to the east.

When Frank Royce was a child, there had been no artificial satellites in the sky, and damn few airplanes. Except for occasional celestial events like a meteor shower, the heavens had remained relatively still. Comfortingly still, in retrospect.

He remembered a gypsy legend. Gypsy children were told not to point out shooting stars but to watch them silently, because each one represented the soul of a fleeing thief. If you pointed out a shooting star, a thief would be caught. So, what if you pointed out a satellite? Who would get caught? A crooked politician?

Interesting legend. It meant the gypsies sided with the thieves, whoever they were. Thieves were good guys. Thieves were . . . innocent? No, not innocent. Just ... good guys. No. One of us? Yes. Good? Innocent? Not necessarily. Just one of us.

For some reason, he felt like crying. He sighed heavily, leaned against the pickup, drank whiskey and watched the stars.

Royce hadn't heard the cricket when it started up again. When he noticed it whirring, he took up the Gladstone bag and started toward the house. The cricket ignored him.

Aha, thought Royce, he's not pointing me out; he's decided I'm one of us; I'm a cricket. Maybe I won't get caught tonight. Every time I come here I gotta start from the ground up.

He'd just gotten inside the door and turned on the hall light when a drinking glass or bottle shattered against the wall next to his face. Bits of glass ticked against his damp shirt and fell on the Gladstone bag at his feet.

Royce paused with his hand on the light switch and took a deep breath. Then he closed the door and turned to face his wife.

He could make out Pamela's form in the darkness, leaning against the jamb of the door that led into the kitchen.

"You're still up," he said quietly.

"No thanks to you," she said.

"Look—" he began.

"I can see," she drawled.

He looked at the bottle in one hand and the bag in the other.

"Been a rough night, Pam."

"It's morning, Royce. Four-thirty o'clock in the morning."

He said nothing.

"Been practicing medicine?" she said archly.

"Not hardly," he said.

"That's an honest answer."

"Let it be, then." He opened the closet door and put his bag in it.

"Said on the television a man died tonight in Huntsville," Pamela said.

Royce closed the closet door and headed for the kitchen.

"Death by injection," she said, as he moved past her. The kitchen was lit by a single low-watt bulb built into the vent over the stove. He found a glass and put some ice in it from the refrigerator.

"Nasty kind of a fellow," Pamela said. "Killed a woman he didn't know for hardly any reason at all."

Makes a saint out of me. He stood looking over the sink at the backyard. "Pamela—"

"Not unless you consider nine dollars a reason to kill somebody."

Here we go. Royce covered the ice with water from the tap and added a couple of inches of whiskey to it. He tapped the top cube down into the mixture and took a sip. Pretty good, but it would be better if it had a chance to cool. Unlikely. He took another sip.

"Some folks kill for a lot more than that, don't they, darling," he said, still watching the darkness out back. Somewhere out there dozed an expensive and nonetheless for it much-neglected quarter horse, broken to an English saddle.

"And just exactly what's that supposed to mean?"

"Nothing, nothing," he said quietly. "I just—"

"If some folks knew how to make a decent living, doing decent work, charging decent wages for it, they wouldn't have to go galavanting all over the countryside killing people to make ends meet. Would they?"

"Not only that—"

"Not only that," she raised her voice, "it's common knowledge that killing a man takes just a minute." She snapped her fingers. "Less than a minute. Then the killer can be on his way, if he's got any sense."

"Not only that," Royce frowned, trying to retain his original line of thought, so he could share it with his wife, "not only that, he wouldn't have to go around killing innocent people...." His voice trailed off. This was going to be difficult to explain, even to someone who wanted to hear it.

Pamela was silent a moment.

Then she said, "That's the most lame, dim-witted, left-field, college-boy excuse I have ever heard out of the mouth of a grown man in all my life."

Royce frowned and turned around. "Beg pardon?"

"I said," she put her hands on her hips, "that's the dumbest, lamest, most off-the-wall excuse I have ever heard!"

Royce frowned. "Excuse?" He spread his arms. "What excuse?"

"That excuse!" she shouted. "You come in here at four-thirty in the morning off a case that was over and done with at midnight sharp in Huntsville, two hours' drive from here, half drunk, and try to throw me off the track with some chicken shit about a tattooed nigger gunslinger being innocent? Or were you suggesting you were innocent yourself? Innocent? I'll show you who's innocent, Franklin Royce. I'm putting out a detective on you!"

Royce couldn't believe his ears. But one look at Pamela and he knew she wasn't lying. She was livid with rage.

"Look, Pamela," he began.

"I'm looking!" she screamed. "You think I'm blind?" She clutched her hands to her breast. "I've been lying here all night—all night!— waiting for you. And this isn't the first time, Royce. No! This hasn't been the first."

"Pam, Pam," he said gently, "you're completely hysterical...."

"I'm not hysterical!" she shouted. "You're an asshole!" She began to cry. "Night after night," she sobbed, "waiting, never knowing where you are, who you're with, why you don't ... why you don't ..."

He'd heard all this before, but there was always the chance she would come up with a new wrinkle. "Why I don't … ?" he coaxed her. "Tell me, darling. Why I don't … ?"

"L-1-love me.…" she sobbed, breaking down.

Not a chance. "There, there," he said, taking a drink.

"Don't touch me, Royce," she said, though he'd made no move to. "I'm not taking this any longer."

Royce swirled the sip of cold whiskey around his teeth.

"I called Daddy …," she said plaintively.

Royce closed his eyes, swallowed the whiskey and stared at the baseboard next to the door. He was very tired. "We get any mail?" he asked idly.

"I told him I was tired, Royce. Tired and lonely and— and scared for our marriage."

Royce sighed. "Naturally he was sympathetic."

"No," she said, looking at him, "no." She shook her head and looked at the floor. "He was shocked, and, and hurt, and surprised, Royce. You know Daddy. He put you through medical school, got us our first place.… He trusts you."

"Yeah," Royce said absently. "He's a good man. But Pamela," he added patiently, "that was twenty-five years ago. We haven't taken a cent off him since. I paid him back for all that twenty years ago. He's been retired for ten years. We've been married for twenty-six years.…"

"But now," she said, "he's not sure about you, Royce.…" Her voice trailed off. "He's just not sure.…"

Royce stared at his wife. He had known her almost all of his life and she was still, in her most tragic moments, very attractive. There was something about tragedy and pain that enlivened her features. Self-concern caused her personality to completely realize her features, to fill them out, and vice versa. Any other subject allowed them to collapse— almost implode—inward upon themselves, to inhabit a gibbering universe full of no-seeums and wing shadows. The death of a star, he mused idly. Somewhere along the line she'd become obsessed with aging. They'd waited a long time to have children; they'd planned very carefully for two of them. But when the time came to begin a family, when they'd bought a very good house and were comfortable in spite of her expenditures, she had balked and stalled. Then she made new promises and set new goals. Then she flatly refused to think about children. Finally, Royce had realized that, all along, she'd been terrified of the idea of children from the beginning, and that somehow she had twisted this terror into some kind of pervasive charm in their lives. And, most curious of all, it worked. On the surface, for years, everything seemed fine. Their daily lives achieved a fine veneer, like a smooth plaster cast. It seemed uniformly solid enough, until you looked beneath its surface, where it became a rigid complex of twisted bandages, swathing something increasingly unpleasant, unrecognizable.

It hadn't even occurred to Royce to force her to have children, but her terror increased unreasonably until one day she came home with her tubes tied. Just like that. Royce went into shock for six months. Then, the children long forgotten, safely avoided, she had become afraid of everything else. She was afraid to drive a car more than a year old. She was afraid to eat meat; she was afraid not to eat meat. She was afraid to eat cheese. She was afraid of Royce. She couldn't stand to be in the same house with him; she was afraid to be alone.

One day he realized he no longer knew this woman who was his wife, and moreover, he no longer cared to know her, whoever she was. Yet, they were married.

"He says …" She clutched her face.

Royce had long since become inured to Pamela's theatrics, but they made it difficult to have a serious conversation with her. There'd been a time, however, when he was amused by them.

"He says?"

She lowered her hand and looked directly at him. "He says he's going to put a detective onto you."

Royce stared at her. Pamela's father was well into his eighties. At one time the two men had been good friends; old man Cotrell had been like a father to Royce. But that had been twenty years ago.

"Pamela," Royce said evenly, "is this on the level?"

"I tried to stop him," she said quickly, "but what could I do?" She wrung her hands. "You know I can't tell Daddy anything. He just insisted. I tried to reason with him. I told him we—you and I—we could work things out. I said we could go away somewhere, just the two of us, maybe down to, to Cabo, or Puerto Vallarta. Oh, Frank … ," and she took his head and tried to lay it on her bosom.

"Can it," Royce said, twisting out of her grasp. He turned to the sink and topped off his glass with more whiskey, skipping the water.

"But he wouldn't be persuaded," she hissed. "No, on the contrary, he insisted. 'I know this is going to be hard on you Pamela,' he said to me, 'and you know I don't like butting in on your affairs. But if that doctor of yours is cheating on you, we'd best find out about it. And when we do, why, then,'" she hesitated, "'then …'"

"Yeah," Royce said, draining half his glass so quickly that its rim tapped sharply against his front teeth. "Then you'll give me a divorce, right?" He lowered the glass and turned to look at her.

A curious light came into Pamela's eyes, but it wasn't as strange as the expression that crawled over the rest of her face.

"Then," she said, "then we'll know who she is, this adultress, who keeps you out drinking and God knows what all, eroding your character, until four-thirty in the morning." She threw the time at him as if it were a damning accusation. "Spending all your money, leeching all your energy, ruining your career, destroying our marriage …"

Suddenly Royce was drunk, very drunk, and very tired. His wife's face was distorted. Her speech was loud and confused. He couldn't grasp the meaning of the words she was using. It was almost as if he couldn't hear her. He could hear her, of course; she was practically screaming. Years ago, he might have spent an hour reassuring her, calming her down until she would take a sedative, and then talking to her soothingly until she fell asleep, and he would put her to bed. But that effort had gradually faded. The years had worn him down. And besides, what difference did it make? He'd lately begun to admit to himself that she was pretty far gone. They'd long since ceased to live together as husband and wife. What had originally been intended as a child's bedroom had long since become his own bedroom. He hadn't minded, really; it was adjacent to the library. So long as he was in the house she didn't bother him much, and they rarely crossed paths at night. Once in a blue moon ...

It was the blue moons that nearly killed him. No rhyme, no reason, not even the full of the moon, but off she would go; for days at a time life was hell for them both, and he was afraid to leave her alone in the house. Often, the fact that he had left her alone in the house would set her off, but that never completely explained it. Nonetheless, the fact that he didn't like to leave her alone had played the devil with his medical practice. It wasn't all her fault, of course. His drinking didn't help things either. He'd done quite well, once. Now ...

That's why he'd quietly taken the corrections job. A few days a week at the prison, tending stab wounds and rape victims. Then this execution business.

Naturally, she'd found out. She knew everything, such as there was to know. Everything but the truth.

He'd never cheated on her. Not once.

Sure, he'd been tempted. But he hadn't. Somehow, in spite of everything, though it had been years since they'd slept together, he hadn't taken up with any other women.

What a fool he'd been.

He looked at her, Pamela, his lovely wife. Her hideous jaws chewed the air, *braying* at him; his wife was *braying*.

For the second time that night he felt the unfamiliar sensation of tears rising in his eyes. He'd loved her once. Perhaps he still did. He'd never cheated on her, never, never, never.

He wondered if she knew that. And suddenly, looking at her in the bleary half-light of the kitchen, he realized that she probably knew damn well how it was. All this stuff about detectives and adultery and her eighty-seven-year-old senile daddy ... But that didn't stop her.

Nothing was going to stop her.

Least of all her beloved husband.

Her beloved husband, least of all ...

Royce stumbled out of the kitchen into the hallway and opened the closet door. He fell against it, and it in turn slammed against the front door as he leaned to pick up the Gladstone bag. When he had the bag and his balance he turned and made for his bedroom. He heard the crash of dishes and glasses in the kitchen. She had long since destroyed their wedding china; they only bought cheap sets of glasses and dishes now, every couple of months. Besides, that was all they could afford. Business was bad; Royce's heart wasn't in it; he spent too much time drinking or at home to build up a good practice. That's why he'd taken the corrections contract. Pick up a few extra bucks.

Then they'd offered him four hundred dollars to be present while they executed Prisoner 61-204.

When he got to his bedroom he locked himself in with the bag. If the bag was safe with him, she could do herself no harm by it. He'd learned that the hard way, a long time ago. He'd forced her to vomit the pills out of her stomach himself, right there in the front hall, next to the closet where he'd kept the bag as long as they'd owned the house. The stain was still on the carpet. Ever since, in his worst moments, every six months or so, a little voice would remind him of that desperate resuscitation, taunting him, asking him why he'd bothered....

And yes, he was afraid of her. That's why he locked the bedroom door every night, in his own house.

A few drinks and he could get some sleep. A good lock and he could be sure he'd wake up.

He'd learned that the hard way, too.

· SIX ·

Royce wasn't sure what woke him up so early the next morning, but was surprised that anything short of a rattlesnake with its tongue in his ear could do it. The hangover was bad, but it was a little better than the day's prospects, like most days. This information had long since become subliminal, and usually allowed him to drink long and hard, sleep long and hard, booze and snooze. It wasn't until standing at the kitchen sink and draining his second tall glass of tap water that he realized what must have happened.

He could see the driveway and the front end of his pickup from where he stood, off to the side of the house. Red plastic lay on the cement below the bumper, where he'd crushed her taillight lenses earlier this morning. Her car was gone. But shards of white glass mingled with the red ones on the pavement, and, without leaning over too much, he could see she'd done a little work on his truck on the way out. It would be just like her to notice the broken taillights right off, the paranoid bitch. Tit for tat, a headlight for a taillight lens …

An eye for an eye. Punitive reciprocity.

He had a very bad headache. Sound and light fired through his brain the way deep, mile-long cracks shoot through pack ice.

She had destroyed the kitchen, or rather, most of the stuff in it. Pieces of glass and crockery were everywhere; he had to put his shoes on to get safely to the sink. She'd even torn an upper cabinet door half off its hinges, and one piece of Formica showed the traces of being clawed by desperate fingernails, or a fork. Looking at the room, he could practically hear the Wagner in her mind. If the cops had walked in at that moment, they'd have had him under a hot light in no time, trying to sweat out the location of Pamela's body.

Indeed, he wished he did know where she was buried.

But that kind of thinking had never gotten him anywhere and

never would. Or, more precisely, he'd never followed up on it. And never would.

Right?

He drew a third glass of water and took it with him to his desk in the library. There he chased down some aspirin. The answering machine tape was blank, as it almost always was. Business was bad; social contacts were nonexistent. The conversation he'd had in the bar on the way home last night was the longest he'd talked to anyone in a long time without shouting at them. Had that been just last night? This morning?

He looked at the clock. A quarter to twelve. This morning, just barely. It had been a very long one.

He looked around the so-called library. It was all Pamela's stuff now, mostly, and the remnants among his own books, he hadn't been able to sell. Some library. To Royce, it looked like some kind of low-tide mark, and little else, a place of small comfort, soon to be mercifully flooded. Unread medical journals, stacks of *Architectural Digest, Better Homes and Gardens, Horse and Rider* and *National Geographic;* James Michener, Louis L'Amour, Zane Grey, Barbara Cartland and Danielle Steele novels; overpriced videotapes: *Giant, Gone with the Wind, The Last Picture Show, High Noon, Terms of Endearment, Love Story,* lots of Astaire and Rogers.

He stared at the telephone for a few minutes.

Maybe there was still time to do something about this morning.

He dialed the prison at Huntsville and got Johanson's secretary on the line. This was an old trusty that nobody except Johanson trusted.

"Thurman."

"Doctor Royce?"

"Got that computer in front of you?"

"You mean my window onto the world, Dr. Royce?" Thurman used the prison's office computer to effectively maintain his self-image as a globe-trotting socialite in a Noel Coward farce entitled *Maximum Security.* Also for blackmail and self-aggrandizement.

"The very same, Thurman," Royce sighed, pinching his hangover by its sinuses. "Right here, Dr. Royce."

"What country are you in, and who's paying the phone bill?"

"Oh, Dr. Royce, you know this modem is so expensive to use I had to requisition a private line just to get me as far as the corrections network right downstairs. Yes, they're so generous down there, and terribly busy. All that dreadfully urgent reform work, you know."

"Yes, I—"

"But since you ask, I'm currently heavily on-line with a delicious little software pirate from Tangier. Dr. Royce, do you know I believe the little piece of goods is lying to me about his age? He says he's just thirteen, and bought himself his own little old hard disc machine with his very own money—they call dollars *dirhams* there—which he scrupulously saved from turning tricks in the Medina. And ever since then he's been off the street and on his keyboard, stealing and dealing software all over the world. All that and only thirteen. Isn't that just about the finest Horatio Algiers tale-of-success story you ever heard?"

Royce agreed that it just about was.

"And," Thurman continued, "he asks me for advice. And I don't mean just computer advice, Dr. Royce. In fact, Dr. Royce—oh!—Dr. Royce, *what* an opportunity! Oh my goodness, I'm so flustered I can barely make myself plain! It seems that Abdhul—that's the boy's name, Abdhul, isn't it just too genuine?—has this little infection, Dr. Royce...."

And Thurman proceeded to describe, in precise detail, a rather intimate problem. Royce listened patiently, then told him what he could do about it. There was no way to determine, with Thurman, precisely who had this problem, as he was not one to lay on the subterfuge too thinly. For all Royce knew, it could have been Johanson himself.

"A few *dirhams* at the local pharmacy, Thurman, that's all it amounts to."

"Oh, Dr. Royce, I can hardly bring myself to merely thank you, sir. Might there be something I could, you know, *do* for you? Hmmmm? Would you like an appointment?"

Royce shook his head. Thurman was doing three consecutive ninety-nine-year terms for burying quite a few young Mexican boys under his Corpus Christi mansion after performing unspeakable things upon them. But that wasn't why Royce politely declined the offer. "No," Royce said, "I don't believe you need to do anything much for me, Thurman, although I was looking to talk to Warden Johanson about something."

"Why, I do thank you, Dr. Royce, and please remember that I'm deeply in your debt. But I'm afraid the Warden is not in his office today...."

Royce already knew that. It was the custom for everyone involved in an execution to take a little time off afterward. Today Johanson would be castrating calves and shooting skeet on his ranch.

"You know, there was an execution this morning, and that *dreadful* murder ..."

"Yes," Royce said tersely, "yes, there was an execution this morning."

"Oh I am sorry, Dr. Royce...."

Like hell.

"We all know how you feel about those dreadful things and I can only say that I thank my lucky stars they caught me in 1970, while that mean old death penalty was out having lunch...."

Indeed, Dr. Royce thought, indeed.

"Not to mention," Thurman prattled on, "it was only after I came here to Huntsville that I learned that Joan Crawford had made so many *wonderful* movies...."

Royce shook his head sadly. Just exactly, he wondered, was the meaning of the word, "carefree"?

"But maybe it's something I can help you with, Dr. Royce?"

"Well, to tell the truth, Thurman," Royce said quickly, "it was just a bit of information I needed, about that fellow last night, I mean, this morning, Bob—I mean," Royce searched his memory, "Robert Lambert Men ... Was it Mencken, that fellow's name, Thurman?"

Thurman sighed. "We called him Snowball, Dr. Royce, those of us that were fond of him."

"Snowball?"

"Pretty humpy, Dr. Royce," Thurman tittered, "if you know what I mean."

"Snowball … ," Royce said thoughtfully.

Thurman's voice took on an oddly pedagogical tone. "Have you never read, Dr. Royce, have you never read Jean Genet's *Miracle of the Rose?*"

"Can't say as I have, Thurman." Like many cons with nothing but time on their hands and an aggressive librarian just a few floors down, Thurman had thoroughly educated himself in the last decade or so. Admittedly, his education reflected a certain bias.

"*Well,* Dr. Royce, *Miracle of the Rose* is a novel, you see, a prison novel—you do know that Genet is one of our great prison novelists?"

Although he'd always heard Genet described as a homosexual novelist, Royce, never having read the man's work, was only marginally aware that Genet had done most of his writing in prison. Primarily, Royce was of a generation that might dimly remember the great outcry from the world's artists and intellectuals that had freed Genet from a life sentence.

"Fag, too—wasn't he?"

"Oh, *absolutely,* Mary," Thurman said archly. "You try making it in the joint otherwise. When they say you're going to do a *stretch,* they—"

"Thurman," Royce said pointedly, "I'm the doctor. Remember?"

"Oh, of course, Dr. Royce, excuse me, I was getting a little giddy.… Oh!" Thurman laughed, "where was I?"

"You said that Mencken was called Snowball?"

"Of course, and aptly yclept, what a dish. In the novel, to go your bail on the five hundred pages, Snowball was a murdering black Adonis, condemned to death, with whom the narrator falls in love. From afar, of course, I hasten to add."

"From afar. You mean from across the exercise yard?"

"Yes!" Thurman enthused. "Exactly, Dr. Royce! Are you sure you didn't read the novel in your, ahm, formative years?"

"Positive."

"So one day the narrator, who's mad for this big, beautiful, black murderer," Thurman savored each of his adjectives unconscionably, as if they were big, new, glass marbles in his front jeans pocket, "has this vision. Snowball is always wreathed in chains, you see, and Genet has built up this delicious, detailed fantasy about him, and lives, fantasizing, from sighting to sighting, as it were, until one day, as he's watching Snowball worshipfully, he sees Snowball's chains turn into garlands of roses! Isn't that beautiful? Because he's a saint, you see, blessed and beatified by Genet's vision...."

"So what's all this to do with Mencken?"

"Nothing, really," Thurman sighed wistfully. "That was the miracle of the rose, you see, the chains turning into roses, the metamorphosis of pure evil into pure beauty, and that's where we got Snowball's nickname...."

"Was he, ahm, saintly, Thurman?"

"Oh, absolutely, Dr. Royce, *divine* is not too strong a word. Why, just this morning in the shower a fellow was observing how in a more perfect world Snowball's shit would be commended to the pope, for beatification, for the single act alone of ridding us of that nasty sociopath, Pit Bull Peters...."

"Has anyone ... claimed the body, Thurman?"

"Whose? Peters'?"

"No, Snowball's."

"I would," Thurman said demurely, "given the—"

"Come on, answer the question," Royce snapped.

"O.K., O.K., keep your blouse on. No; the answer's no."

"Did he ever have any visitors?"

By the timbre of the silence coming over the phone, Royce could tell that Thurman was pouting.

"Thurman, look ... You liked Bob—I mean Snowball." Thurman spoke with a catch in his voice. "I, I loved him, Doctor...."

I take back what I thought about carefree, Royce reflected sourly. "Would you give me a little help on this? It might ... I don't know...." Royce looked at the wall of medical journals beyond his desk. Might as well come straight out with it. He might surprise himself as much as Thurman. But a moment passed before he said, "I want to find out what happened to him."

Thurman didn't seem too surprised. "Don't you think it's a little late to be looking into Snowball's case, Dr. Royce?" His tone was decidedly cool.

"No," Royce said thoughtfully. "I don't think so."

Thurman was silent a moment. Then he said, "Hang on."

Royce swiveled his old chair around so he could look through the sliding glass door that led to the side yard, where the pool was always going to be, where nothing but an old rusted-out Aeromotor windmill always had been. What he looked out on was a vast plain of mesquite and tumbleweeds and post oak, distinguishable from his property by a barbed wire fence running through it about thirty yards from the house. A hawk circled in the distance, high above the gentle rise a half-mile to the south.

Royce could hear the distinctive clicks and beeps of a computer keyboard. After a long minute, Thurman spoke. "Do you have a computer handy, Dr. Royce?"

Royce turned around and faced his desk. "There's an old Underwood portable in front of me."

"MS-DOS?"

"Yes." The world is leaving me behind, he thought.

"Right on. Does it have a modem?"

He fingered the shift key on the typewriter. The carriage moved up and down. "There's one built in."

"Boot it up," Thurman said glibly. "You'll need about 50K for the file—"

"Thurman—"

"He was a beautiful man, Dr. Royce. I'll print the file and leave it in your box."

· SEVEN ·

The tall young black man's head was shaved as close and smooth as an eight ball, and his wraparound sunglasses fit him so closely they looked like they'd been leaded into his face, like a taillight in the fender of a customized car. When he turned to point the way, the top of his head showed where the stylist had bleached white a perfect circle of closely cropped, tightly curled hair around a pair of circles left black, one above but overlapping the other, to form the numeral eight. He held his head high and stood perfectly straight, and didn't mind at all telling Royce how to find number sixteen Zapata Street, in a very deep voice. They were standing on Zapata Street at the time. But number sixteen faced onto an unnamed dead-end alley off the north side of the middle of the block. The numbering simply came down the street, ran up one side of the alley and back down, and continued another two blocks west, toward the Oak Hill district. It was a simple thing to have missed. Anyone might have missed it. But missing it made Franklin Royce nervous. He felt compelled to make a friendly overture to this kid, almost as tall as he was, who had shown himself willing to be friendly.

"Thank-you, son," he said pleasantly. "What's your name?"

The young man tilted his head forward and pointed to the spot of hair on top. "Eight Ball," he said.

Royce smiled and proffered a dollar bill at the kid. The kid looked at it.

"I'm not a cop or anything," Royce explained.

The kid squinted myopically. "You telling me, mister?"

"So take the dollar."

Eight Ball waited.

Royce shrugged. "The lady lives at sixteen, you know her?"

Eight Ball grinned. "Sheeeee…"

"How's that?"

"Everybody knows her."

"Is her name Colleen?"

"Yeah. Her name's Colleen."

"Lived there three, maybe four months?"

The kid screwed up his face and asked him, "Hey, mister, why don't you go down to the gas station and talk to the mirror in the washroom? It'll sound just the same as you standing there asking me questions you already know the answers to."

"Take the buck, kid. Go buy some chalk for your cue."

Eight Ball looked at him thoughtfully for a moment; then he smiled and took the dollar. "I have been scratching lots," he said cheerfully.

Royce watched the kid lope down the middle of the street. He walked with his long arms straight down at his sides and very stiff-legged, using the full hinge action of each foot instead of his knees to make it from one stride to the next. He'd had something with that remark about the mirror. Royce had stopped looking into them awhile back and wasn't planning on looking into another one any time soon. He didn't like to see the pudginess his drinking had gradually brought into his face, or the traces of blood in the whites of his eyes, or the burst vessels just beneath the mottled surface of the skin of his nose… any more than he liked to be reminded of the first time a barber had offered to dye his hair back to brown—or black, even. He picked up the Gladstone bag and made his way up the street. He passed two men staring sadly into the engine compartment of a parked car. Each had a hand on the raised hood and a foot up on the front bumper. Various tools lay along a length of carpet padding draped along the streetside fender. Children of all ages ran up and down the block, chasing a ball, chasing each other, seemingly oblivious to the evening heat and humidity. An old yellow dog lay across the sidewalk in the shade of the building that stood at the mouth of the alley that opened onto Zapata Street, with his head up on the dusty sidewall of a bald tire. He was breathing deeply and slowly, his rheumy eyes half-closed and his red tongue spilling out of the side of his mouth.

Royce turned into the alley and found a worn set of wooden stairs going up the face of a three-story wood-frame building with clapboard siding and yellow paint peeling off of it. Two pot-metal numerals, a one and a six, painted the same color as the building, were tacked to a post that supported the outside of the staircase. A lot of broken glass and empty potato-chip bags had accumulated beneath the first run of stairs. Some local entrepreneur would be keeping the place free of anything aluminum. A stripped motorcycle frame sat rusting on its forks among the trash under the stairs, secured by lock and chain to the same post that held up the address.

Royce climbed to the first landing and faced a bewildering profusion of doorbell buttons set into a piece of plywood nailed across a gate that more or less blocked further access to the building, although any kid wouldn't have much trouble getting around it. One step up onto the banister and security was history. In fact, it looked so easy to bypass any courtesy about getting into this place that he had another thought and pressed the gate. It swung back on its hinges with no resistance whatsoever, just a creak.

She lived all the way up in the back, and took a long time answering his knock. When she did, Royce wondered why or how she'd bothered.

Colleen Valdez was so stoned when she opened the door she could barely stand. She had raven-black hair that fell straight to her waist, with a few tangles on the way, and wore an apricot housecoat that enclosed more or less of her hair in more or less the same proportions as it exposed her body. Even though she was speaking to her unexpected visitor, her eyes were closed, and that was that. Her voice was just a little louder than an interior monologue, and said about the same thing. She smacked her lips gently between the words she was using. As she muttered, Royce watched a thin trickle of blood as it crept down the inside of her forearm.

"Oh, Eddie," she said, "I, uh, mean..."

"Excuse me, ma'am," Royce said, doffing his short-brim, "I'm a friend of Bobby Mencken's, and I'm looking for a Miss Colleen

Valdez?"

A small frown flitted across her blank features, as if she were blind and couldn't remember where she'd left the salt shaker. "Oh, wow," she said, and smiled briefly and might have batted her lashes but couldn't get her eyes to completely open, "a real gentleman. Well I swan. But... she's not... She's... *indisposed* you see...." She swallowed and made the light smacking sound with her lips, as if they were quite dry, flicked the tip of her tongue over them. Then she began to shake her head and said as if to herself, "I don't even know why I answered the door," and giggled slightly, effortlessly, as if there were not enough energy in her system to get out a really decent laugh, even if the joke were on herself, and then she frowned like a little girl. Royce thought the joke might have been on her. If he'd been a cop he might have run this girl in on a narcotics charge. As it was he said, "You don't seem particularly well, Miss Valdez. May I help you to a chair?"

Miss Valdez took a deep breath that evidently taxed her strength beyond its capacity, for it caught in her throat on the way in, and she blanched completely white. Then she sagged against the doorpost, turned around it and fell into Royce's arms.

She weighed maybe 110 pounds. Royce dropped his bag and his Stetson to catch her. "Miss Valdez?" No answer. He carried the woman into the apartment. The front door opened into a narrow hallway. Going left, he found himself in a very small and very disorganized kitchen, with the smell of burnt matches in the air. He backed down the hall and out the front door, turned and made for the right-hand end of the apartment. Here he found two rooms. In the first were a ragged overstuffed chair, a guitar, a sofa and a table facing a television set on a small bureau. In the second a splintered double-hung window looked over a patchwork of backyards and clotheslines and a teeming freeway a quarter- or half-mile away. A tangled double bed took up nearly the entire room, and he awkwardly laid the woman down on it as gently as possible. He took her pulse. It was slow but regular. He checked her arms and found tracks running up and down both of them. There was a little barrel serving as a table beside the bed. On it lay an eyedropper fitted with the bulb of a child's pacifier at one end and a hypodermic needle at the other, with a trace of blood still on its point; a bent spoon that had been burned black; several blackened matches; a candle end, still burning; a half-empty matchbook; a razor blade. A glassine envelope on top of a paperback copy of *War and Peace* had been slit open along its seams and smoothed flat. It was the kind of tiny translucent envelope stamp collectors used to get their rare issues in. Maybe they still do.

Interesting, Royce thought. He blew out the candle.

The room was very close. He drew a ragged piece of cloth over the open window and the room became dark. A thick, humid atmosphere of jungle congress subsumed it. There was a broomstick cutting across the corner of the room at the foot of the bed, from one nail in one wall to another nail in the window sash, with a bunch of clothes hanging from it on hangers or draped carelessly over it: a man's clothes and a woman's clothes, flowered patterns on thin fabrics, worn out and faded from being so loud for so long.

He sat on the edge of the bed with his back to the window and watched the drugged woman for a while.

It was her face that got him first. It was evenly mottled by smallpox scars, or some disfigurement like them; her face was ruined. It looked like pitted marble, five hundred years old. But like Bobby Mencken, she was young, not yet thirty. But it could have been beautiful. In fact, the more Royce looked at Colleen Valdez' face the more he came to think of it as beautiful. Her complexion was slightly browned, whether by sun or blood he couldn't know. But her eyes were narrow, as if from an Asian influence, and the scarred cheekbones close up under them. The nose was small and straight, slightly rounded. Though now drained of their color, her lips were full but wide over surprisingly even little teeth, between which he could see the tip of her pink tongue.

And she had many of the other feminine attributes men think a matter of beautification. Breasts, hips and thighs swelled appropriately beneath the taffeta housecoat. Dark hair sparsely swept along her bare arms like gently curved, fragile filaments aligned by secret magnetic fields. Her calves folded together like parallel waves, glided very nicely into two perfectly bare, finely arched feet. Her face swathed in raven hair lay on the pillow like a bust of a pale Madonna packed in a nest of fine ebony excelsior.

By God, Royce thought, this indeed is a very fine specimen of a woman. And suddenly his mind was cast back over thirty years, to an anatomy class, and the cadaver he'd shared there with three other students. The body had once been a young woman, killed in a motorcycle accident, unaccountably donated to science. And they'd all wondered who she was, what she'd done, how she'd moved, thought, acted, lived and ... Well. They knew how she'd died. Multiple internal injuries, severe trauma to the brain, internal and external bleeding, a broken neck...

Now, here was the other side of the coin, Royce thought: a woman who, like the motorcycle girl, has deliberately put herself on the edge of death, yet unlike the other, here she remains, alive; she's going to survive. And I could discover all those things about her before—if and when—she dies.

He thoughtfully placed his middle and ring fingers against the carotid artery in the woman's neck. The pulse was very slow but very regular. Her skin was cool in the hot evening. He stroked the artery, the neck, the underside of her chin. Her pocked skin slid under his fingers like coarse, silky burlap. Yes, a very lovely woman. He could see now what any man might see in her, and that wouldn't exclude Bobby Mencken, who had lived with her for at least two years before he was imprisoned, five or six addresses ago.

He removed his hand from her throat and let it slide along her shoulder, down her arm, over her hip, along the swell of her thigh. Then he removed it.

He went out to the hallway and retrieved the Gladstone bag and his hat. Closing the door behind him, he stashed the bag behind the sofa in the living room and put the hat on the table. It had been a long night, and a long day. After he'd read Mencken's case history, at least insofar as the prison had records of it, he'd packed the file and a few other things into the Gladstone bag and headed out for Dallas without so much as a single look back. The drive was quite long, over eight hours. During it he'd become accustomed to the idea of Bobby Mencken's innocence, and furthermore, he'd become accustomed to the idea that he was going to take a stab at finding out why Mencken had taken the ultimate fall for something he might not have done. What he was going to do if and when he found an answer was something he hadn't quite thought out yet.

Colleen Valdez was his first lead. Her name had once figured on Bobby's visitor list, and she hadn't been too difficult to find. He'd only been searching since yesterday. Everybody remembered the tall beauty with the ruined complexion. Judging by the look of things, she was a little too broke and a little too self-involved to be going down to Huntsville to claim the body. But that wouldn't be bothering Bobby any. In fact, she hadn't been to see him in two years.

Royce left the shabby apartment and walked a couple of blocks until he found a liquor store, where his Spanish was good enough to get him a bottle of Ezra Brooks' Tennessee Sipping Whiskey. Night was coming on for good, but he thought it was as hot and humid as it could conceivably be outside of Houston. He looped around a couple of blocks to get the benefit of the thick air. People were hanging around in the darkness on their stoops, talking quietly among themselves. The men wore sleeveless undershirts or none at all. The women had small children with big eyes on their laps. Everywhere windows were open to the hope of cool air, and here and there he would hear music from a radio or see the blue light of a television dart over the walls of a dark room. Once he passed by his pickup truck. A couple of young kids were playing in the back of it. He chased them away, and they watched him from the end of the block as he saw to it that the truck was still locked. After a while, he made his way back to the apartment, to wait for Colleen Valdez to come down enough to wake up and talk to him.

· EIGHT ·

When he first awoke, Royce couldn't tell how long he'd been asleep. He'd enjoyed one of those naps people take when they've been doing the same thing for too long and have little hope of ever getting around to doing anything else, so they better get rested up for it. Life around them wouldn't have had enough time to change very much while they were napping, but then, life would never get enough time to change at all, so far as these nappers are concerned. So maybe he'd been asleep about an hour.

But things had changed since Royce had fallen asleep, even though he hadn't been asleep very long. Gentle changes. Musical changes. A man, very close to him, was strumming the guitar and singing.

> *The old hometown looks the same*
> *As I step down from the train,*
> *And there to meet me is my mama and papa.…*

Royce kept his eyes closed and listened. A simple melody, but there was a sadness in the voice. A very soothing sadness.

> *Down the road I look and there runs Mary,*
> *Hair of gold and lips like cherries.…*

The singer broke into talking without disturbing the rhythm of his chords. "Hey, hey, Colleen," he said, "that's you, honey," and he laughed and repeated the line; but by the following line his voice had regained its introspection.

> *… hair of gold and lips like cherries.*
> *It's good to touch the green, green grass of home.…*

Royce might have vaguely remembered the tune, but he was strangely touched by the plaintive simplicity of it, and couldn't place the source of its emotion, until the player strummed the instrument around the verse one time, and then took up the lyric again.

> *Then I awake and look around me*
> *At four gray walls that surround me,*
> *And I realize that I was only dreaming....*

Ah, so. A prison song, and a very famous one. One might still find Porter Wagoner's version of it on truck stop jukeboxes in certain parts of the West.

> *For there's a guard and there's a sad old padre.*
> *Arm in arm, we'll walk at daybreak....*

> *Yes, they'll all come to meet me,*
> *Arms reaching, smiling sweetly.*
> *It's good to touch the green, green grass of home....*

The singer repeated the chorus and then began to pick out the melody line on the guitar strings. He found his way through it once, jazzed it up the second time through, and his third version was very hip, according to his own comment mid-chorus, "Yeah." Then he slowed it down and spoke the last verse as he played, the way Wagoner did it.

> *Then I wake and look around me*
> *At four gray walls that surround me*
> *And I realize ... I was only dreaming.*
> *For there's the guard and there's the sad old padre.*
> *And we're gonna walk ...*

Here the player walked the guitar strings,

> *... arm in arm at daybreak....*

Now, with an unexpected fervor that neatly eclipsed his previous fooling around, the player swung into a fine, understated and unbearably sad final chorus.

> Yes, they'll all come to meet me
> In the shade of that old oak tree
> As they lay me 'neath the green, green grass of home....

Then the player, apparently a recidivist clown, vitally strummed the fourth chord, probably a C, and sang with it a long "Ahhhhhhh," as if he were having his tonsils examined, Royce thought. Then he descended onto the tonic like an owl onto a rat, necessarily a G, and sang "Me-ennnnn... ," all the while decreasing the tempo of the strum until he'd decided it was time to end on the final bottom note of the chord, also a tonic G, and did so.

Amen, agreed Royce, what a relief.

"And if that didn't wake you up, mister, you're dreaming you're sleeping in church."

Royce opened one eye. The guitarist was sitting in the sagging easy chair opposite the end of the sofa Royce had stretched out on. Half of him was bathed in the flickering blue light of the television, the only light in the room, by which it could be seen that he was shirtless and tattooed. Prison tattoos. A scorpion, spiders, little knives, a woman in tears, a 13, a 69. Black and blue tattoos on the bluish-white skin. His head had been shaved but the white hair had been coming back for a while, and the tattoos on his skull looked like the reforested landscape diagrams of Nazca. The skull itself was so narrow and fleshless it had the warped uncial figure-eight appearance of the screaming bedlamite's in Edvard Munch's famous picture, "The Scream," with a shiny star-shaped puncture scar on his left cheek. His bare arms were very thin also, but finely muscled, and indeed the guitarist was not a particularly small man. He had long, finely boned fingers that could easily fret the thick, wide neck of the Spanish-style instrument across his lap. Each hand sported a large ring, each of a figured flat stone mounted in silver. These moved fitfully but tunefully over the strings, but the eyes gleaming white, deep in the moist gloom of their sockets, watched Royce.

"Aha," said the guitarist, seeing Royce's open eye, "half dreaming."

Royce moved uneasily in the deep cushions of the couch. His bottle hit the filthy olive-green carpet below with a thump.

"Well, I'll be damned, Colleen," the guitarist whined, "the reverend done dropped his bottle right between hymn number one," he strummed the fourth, "and·hymn number two." He strummed the tonic. "Say, Reverend, how about a little communion for the choir?" He fingered a bright little ditty that had something suspended about it, just the kind of thing one might expect to presage an intermission at a dance. "Mind?"

Royce sat himself up and tried to shake off the effects of his sleep and the two or three stout snorts he'd had beforehand. He picked up the bottle and looked at it—two-thirds full—and passed it over.

"My, my," said the guitarist, "Ezra Brooks. That's good whiskey, Reverend."

Royce rubbed his head with both hands and asked what time it was.

"Nighttime," said the guitarist, lifting the bottle.

"The right time," Royce muttered, just to be friendly.

The guitarist swallowed and raised an eyebrow. "Always the right time around here," he said, handing the bottle back to Royce.

Royce had assumed his standard television posture. He was sitting on the edge of the sofa, leaning forward, his forearms resting on his knees, a bottle nearby, the screen flickering before him. The flicker appealed to his grogginess.

The guitarist picked idly for a few minutes. Royce saw a package of cigarettes on the table and held it up. The guitarist nodded. Royce lit one and watched the television awhile. There was something soothing about the television, something that postponed the future, or suspended the present, and after noticing that, Royce found himself staring at it without prejudice, sure that everyone would understand if he didn't want to be interrupted.

The guitarist strummed softly and watched this stranger on the couch. Royce had salt-and-pepper hair cut in a short burr, what was called "GI" after World War II; a sweat-stained, white, short-sleeved shirt with a button-down collar; innocuous tan pants held up by a belt; thin, white socks in unshined brown brogans. A ballpoint pen was in the shirt's breast pocket. He would be about fifty.

A mildly amused expression came over the guitarist's features as he watched Royce. Then he leaned forward over his guitar to have a look at the television screen. A sequence of rapidly cut scenes were selling beer. He looked at Royce. Royce's eyes did not leave the screen. His mouth hung slightly open. The guitarist retrieved the whiskey bottle and sat back in his chair.

"Got a name, Reverend?"

"Royce." He took his eyes off the television. "Franklin Royce." His eyes went back to the screen.

"Call you Frank?"

"Wife called me Royce. When I had a wife."

"How about Rolls Royce? Anybody ever call you Rolls Royce?"

"That's what Bobby called me, once, in a way."

"You and Bobby were partners in stir?"

Royce was silent.

The guitarist took a cigarette, lit it and sat back against the cushions of his chair, the guitar flat in his lap. He blew smoke into the blue gloom. Then he said, "That's the way I feel about the bastards, too. Let 'em eat anonymity."

Royce smiled vaguely at the television.

The guitarist crossed his legs. "Keep out of their way, I mean," he explained. "If they don't even know what to call you, they can't come and find you. They don't even know your name. That takes care of all sorts of stuff. Taxes, for example. They can't get any taxes off you if they don't know where to find you, and they don't know where to find you if they don't know who you are. It's a good system. Of course, you have to make certain sacrifices. Like you can't have any credit, or a telephone—at least, not in your own name. That's a whole other scam." The guitarist waggled the bare foot propped over his knee and watched it. "But all in all, it's a good system. That's why we ain't got a phone here. I was thinking," he added abruptly, "about getting somebody to tattoo some rattles on this foot of mine, and a snake head on the back of my neck with his mouth wide open, so my face is in his mouth, connected by a long series of diamondback rattlesnake type designs curling around my spine and through the crack of my ass and 'round and around my leg, until it gets to my foot, where the rattles are, and that's where the snake's tail would be, see, and I could sew a bunch a dried seed pods to my sneakers or maybe to just the webbing between my toes, and then I'd completely realize my snakeness and at the same time get people off my back about why I waggle this foot all the time." He blew smoke in Royce's direction. "That's my totem, the rattlesnake. You know?"

After a moment Royce moved his head in the guitarist's direction with a series of wooden movements. He looked at him a moment, said "Sure," and looked back at the television.

"Of course," the guitarist continued, "it'd have to be a really good tattoo artist, you know, maybe Erno out on the coast, the kinda guy who wouldn't mind sleeping with a few snakes just to get their moves down right, making a really close study of them, because after all a snake of these huge proportions would have to be exact, right down to the smallest detail, a real artist, a guy that's devoted to the transmogrification of skin."

Royce raised an eyebrow. On the screen, the Cowboys were looking out of whack. He wondered how it could be Monday night.

The guitarist picked a speck of organic matter off the tip of his tongue and studied it as he continued. "But I don't know this guy Erno from Adam. I mean, I heard of him. He's a big tattoo man out there in Frisco, on the coast. There's guys around here that do it, down in Galveston. You gotta have a port city, where there's ships and sailors and stuff, to get a really together tattoo artist. Of course," he shrugged and modulated his voice, "that doesn't exactly limit the possibilities. There's a lotta ports in the world, you know? But as usual, man, you have to be in the scene, man, and have a little bread, you know, man, and a few connections, man, to make sure you don't get some guy who turns your back into the Book of Revelations, man, or a letter to his mother, or a spider that vampires your blood in your sleep...."

Still Royce was locked into the Dallas Cowboys, and why shouldn't he be? He'd had a lot on his mind lately. Pamela is definitely certifiable.... No, let's not get into reality tonight.... Nice pass....

The guitarist regarded Royce with philosophical annoyance. He took two quick drags on his cigarette and set aside the guitar. "The doctor I got on ATD with," he said, leaning forward to crush the butt in the ashtray on the table in front of Royce, "says this thing with the foot is tensions." He took the bottle and leaned back into his chair. He crossed his foot over his knee and it began oscillating again. "I said I'd had them ever since I was a kid." He raised the bottle and had a swallow. "'That's a sure sign of intelligence,' the quack says with a tentative smile. 'No way,' I'm saying to him. 'It goes along with the two hollow teeth in the front of my mouth and the hissing I hear whenever I eat peyote. It's my innate snakeness, Doc. The rattlesnake is my totem. Nothing and nobody is going to convince me any different. I'm a fucking snake, and that's that.' Well." He replaced the bottle on the table between himself and Royce and lit another cigarette. "It wasn't too long after that they decided I was socially 4F, if you know what I mean, and granted me the Aid for the Totally Dependent."

The Cowboys were driving downfield, looking good, and here it was just an exhibition game—in fact it might have been a replay of an exhibition game from last year. Royce felt for the bottle and fitted the neck to his mouth without looking at it.

"They thought I was crazy, and I don't blame them. I'm just glad for all of us that I didn't have to go too far with the whole thing. But crazy is one thing, and thrift is something else. I been saving some of that ATD money. I know, I know," he held up a hand, palm out, "you think that's impossible. After all, ATD's not all that much, and Reagan even cut it back some. Still and all, we get by on the grace of God and miscellaneous felonies." He regarded the end of his cigarette and blew on it. Little bits of ash flew off the end and the coal glowed brightly. "By and by," he continued, taking a small puff and looking at

the end again, "I'm going to have enough to get that tattoo one day."
He looked down at his body. "Get rid of all this big house peacock
shit." He looked at Royce. Royce looked at the television. "Then, by
God," the guitarist said quietly, "then, by God, with that snake body
all coiled around me, when that foot starts to shake," his foot started
to shake, "and the seed pods start to rattle, shake-a shake-a shake-a,
and maybe a little hissssss... people are gonna by God *know.*"

Before Royce knew what hit him, the guitar player had sprung
out of his chair and straddled Royce on the sofa. Royce momentarily
held the man off as if the act were a lame plot hatched merely to interrupt his enjoyment of the football game, keeping the guitarist's body
to one side of him so he could keep his eyes on the screen. But as he
leaped the guitarist shouted, *"By God know that they're fucking with a
by God GEN-u-whine REP-tile!"* and quickly burned two holes right
next to each other on the side of Royce's neck with the red hot end
of his cigarette. The act was so aggressive that Royce's pain took him
completely by surprise and the cigarette had extinguished itself on
his neck under the pressure of the application of the second burn before he reacted.

Royce screamed. He rolled onto the floor between the sofa and
the table, clutching both hands to his neck, curling around the wound
like a fishing worm around the inserted hook.

The guitarist stood away and let him howl. He took a drag on
the cigarette stub, saw it was dead and flicked it toward the writh-
ing creature at his feet, laughing. "Man," he said, "you been snake-
bit." He leaned toward Royce and tapped his shoulder with his fist.
"Fast Eddie Lamark's the name," he leered, "and gen-u-whine reptile
trauma is my game."

He picked up the bottle just as Royce kicked the table hard
enough to turn it over, and took a long swallow.

· NINE ·

Eddie Lamark finished the whiskey and considered the bottle. Then he threw it through the television.

The tube imploded with a dull thud, like a door slamming in a distant room, and went black. The sound of the football game continued around the fumes drifting up out of the jagged hole, as if narrating an obscure contest between minerals. Then there was a spitting sound and the narration faded to nothing. A bluish color flickered over the face of the jagged glass, like distant heat lightning. Being an unhappily married prison doctor, Royce had witnessed a fair amount of violence in his time, but when he'd been its victim, it hadn't been random; and when it had been random, he'd never been its victim. Therefore, after Royce stood up, twisting around the small room with both his hands covering the twin burns on his neck, and asked what the hell it'd all been done to him for, he wasn't too surprised when Eddie gave him raised eyebrows, took a beat, then shrugged and shook his head. But Royce was nonetheless mad, and Eddie Lamark's honest shrug only further enraged him; so, still holding onto his neck with one hand, he took a swing at Lamark with the other. He missed. Lamark retaliated by burying his fist in Royce's stomach. It was a deep, satisfying hit that dropped the older man to his knees. Then Lamark backed off as inexplicably as he'd begun. Royce knelt on the ragged carpet, struggling to hold down the eighty-six-proof bile that threatened to choke him as he gasped for his wind. He was in a perfect position; Lamark might have dealt him a blow to the side of his head that might well have killed him.

Instead, Lamark stood back and lit a cigarette. One drag, two. He blew smoke at the match, but the match didn't go out. Then he leaned forward a bit and grabbed Royce by the chin. He twisted it roughly and contemplated Royce's face by matchlight.

"Who the fuck are you, mister?" The playfulness was all gone from his voice.

Royce was hurt and could not breathe well and didn't want to answer that question, but he suddenly guessed that Lamark was going to set him on fire. With a yell he twisted away from the match, fell against the sofa and onto the floor.

Eddie Lamark showed some teeth with a smile. A curl of smoke lifted out of his open mouth. He breathed smoke at the match until it went out.

Royce cowered on the floor in the darkness. His thoughts went to the Gladstone bag he'd hidden behind the sofa. There he'd find an unguent for the burns and enough sodium thiopental to freeze Lamark's leer into a death mask. Never before had Royce so strongly felt the hatred that overwhelmed him now, not even in his worst nights with Pamela. In ten minutes Lamark had succeeded in releasing years of confusion and frustration, and simultaneously focused himself as the sole and most accessible object by which Royce might obtain some relief. Royce used this hatred to face down his pain and strive for reason. His breath whistled through his clenched teeth.

Through the court transcripts and other materials he'd found in Thurman's file, Royce was fairly convinced that Lamark and Colleen Valdez had been very close to Bobby Mencken at the time of the convenience store robbery and murder for which Mencken had been put to death. The prosecutor's case had been strong but highly circumstantial. Mencken had been nabbed fleeing the scene. The murder weapon turned up nearby with Mencken's prints all over it. Valdez and Lamark had been interviewed a week or so later, but nothing came of it. They were each other's alibis. Mencken took the rap.

But Royce couldn't forget the man's eyes the night he helped him die. Mencken had been innocent.

Anyway, Royce was operating on that theory.

He thought "operating" was kind of a loose term.

Royce sat up in the corner between the couch and the wall. He licked two fingers and pressed them over the two burns on his neck and waited in the darkness. Across the tiny room he could see the glow of Lamark's cigarette. It would be damn hard to believe that Mencken had taken the fall for this Eddie guy. Not if this was his normal behavior, and Royce had no reason to think the man ever behaved otherwise.

The girl, though. She might once have been worth taking a risk for. But a sacrifice?

It was then that Royce remembered the two round disks of shiny scar tissue on Mencken's shoulder. Now Royce lay cowering on the floor in a Dallas tenement with his fingers pressed painfully to two wounds that, when healed, would look just like them.

He would be wearing Eddie Lamark's brand.

Just like Bobby Mencken.

A yellow overhead light suddenly illuminated the room.

"What's going on in here?"

Colleen Valdez stood in the bedroom door to Royce's right, hugging herself in her taffeta robe and looking very sleepy. She scratched her head with one hand and looked at Royce, then passed her eyes over the wreckage of the room until they found Eddie, who stood against the opposite wall. "What time is it?" she yawned.

"Time to get a new bottle of whiskey and a new television," Eddie said. "Where you been?"

"Oh, man," she said through the yawn. "I just took a shot that reminded me why I became such useless trash in the first place." As she spoke she leaned over and righted the table blocking the doorway. "Anyway, I think it did," she added. "The last thing I remember is this guy here," she pointed to Royce, "catching me when I passed out in the hallway. Thanks."

Royce nodded, not taking his eyes off Lamark.

Pause.

"So," she said, taking the last cigarette out of a package on top of the ruined television. She eyed the broken neck of the whiskey bottle protruding from the hole in the picture tube and added, "Looks like we're getting all our vices in one place, here."

"So let's go get a bottle and a television," Eddie said, not taking his eyes off Royce. "Who is this guy, anyway?"

Colleen Valdez turned her head and held a match to her cigarette. "Said he was a friend of Bobby Mink's," she said, waving out the match.

"Stir?" Lamark asked.

Royce said nothing, but he was pleasantly surprised to hear that Colleen Valdez was able to remember meeting him earlier that afternoon.

"Don't fight like he was in stir," Lamark observed.

"I'm an intellectual," Royce said defensively.

Lamark flexed the fingers of his punching hand, opening and closing them as he watched Royce through the smoke of the cigarette in his mouth.

"Is that the same thing as smart?" Colleen asked absently, looking for an ashtray for her match. Though moving a little on the slow side, she was markedly more alert than the first time Royce had met her, and correspondingly more interesting to look at. She was much taller than Royce had thought her at first. She gave up on the ashtray and flipped the dead match onto the table. "That's the kind Bobby liked."

"Funny time to be showing up," Lamark said, "Bobby going down just day before yesterday and all. Why here?"

"I came to find out how civilized people behave themselves," Royce said. "Figured any friend of Bobby's would know all about it."

Lamark laughed.

"Fucking and fighting," Colleen said as she headed for the kitchen. "Nothing's changed." Royce and Eddie watched each other. Royce had gotten his wind back now and thought he was sailing pretty well around any hard facts that might have tripped him up. He realized, though, that he would have to be delicate in the matter of introducing these people to the contents of his Gladstone bag. Undoubtedly, there were some items in there that they would be wanting to consume right away. The morphine, for example, would save the likes of these two the trouble of hitting the streets for at least a couple of days.

A sense of having found an edge to the prevailing chaos of this new environment infused a bit of much-needed calm into the panicked helplessness threatening Royce's presence of mind. Though the morphine was undoubtably a playable card, he had few illusions as to whether Lamark or even the girl might not kill him for it if he played it wrong.

He felt like a tourist in Manhattan, speaking no English, who suddenly wakes up to the fact that it's 3:00 A.M. on a Tuesday, and he's wandering around Times Square wearing suspenders and lederhosen and a Miss Liberty T-shirt with a passport and two thousand dollars in traveler's checks sticking out of his back pocket and an expensive camera on a strap around his neck: vulnerable.

But his fear was tinged with excitement. His pain was tempered by the knowledge that the first lead he'd gotten out of the Mencken file had led him straight to at least one person completely capable of having committed the acts for which the state of Texas had held Bobby Mencken responsible.

If he could prove it, Mencken was as good as avenged. Royce looked at Lamark in a new, strange light. Lamark's death might be the vehicle of Mencken's vindication. And now it would be a pleasure to effect it, given the provocation Lamark had just supplied him. Royce would be glad to trade Eddie Lamark a brand for a hot shot. Were such square deals still available on this tangled earth?

The thought occurred to him that if Lamark were as crazy as he acted, all Royce might have to do would be to ask him who killed Amanda Johnson, a mother of five who worked nights in a convenience store at $3.25 an hour to make ends meet. Eddie might tell him.

The thought also occurred to him that this snake Lamark, being crazy and possibly smart, probably wouldn't allow him enough time to find out much of anything. Certainly, guilty or not, he'd managed to be smarter than Mencken. He hadn't gotten caught.

"I hadn't seen Bobby much since he went up to Death Row anyway," Royce offered. "We got to be friends when he was heavily into… physical therapy. Yeah." A pain shot through Royce's gut. He clutched it with both hands and winced. "Physical therapy."

Lamark shook his head very slowly and said, "It's a cinch you aren't into physical therapy, Jack."

Royce closed his eyes and bit his lip against the pain. "I was into the theoretical side of things," he said lamely, although warming to the fabrication, "I was the therapist. Trusty, you understand. I was a doctor outside..."

Lamark frowned slightly. "A doctor?" His lip curled into a sneer. "What kind of doctor?"

Royce shook his head. "Doesn't make any difference. I, uh... I went down writing scrips for upper-class junkies."

Lamark smiled hopefully. "You still got a license?"

Royce laughed. "You mean to drive?"

Lamark shook his head, laughing begrudgingly.

"Anyway," Royce continued, "I was up for parole on account of good behavior and it just so happens I came out a few days ago, right before Bobby Mink..." He let his voice trail off. After a minute he picked up the thread again in a slightly different tone, substituting a slight bitterness for a slight melancholy. "My wife met me at the gate and gave me my old Gladstone bag with some clothes in it. Then the sheriff's deputy with her gave me a summons to divorce court, an injunction not to ever darken the door of my own house again, and the keys and title to my own pickup truck. Then we parted ways. For good, I guess."

Royce noticed the hem of the taffeta housecoat just around the corner of the entry hall, where Colleen Valdez was leaning against the wall smoking a cigarette and listening to his story. The one brown bare foot he could see was small and had a fine arch to it.

Eddie looked at the end of his own cigarette. "And how's old Thurman?" he asked simply.

Royce flicked his eyes from Colleen's foot to Eddie's face. Eddie kept watching his cigarette. In the hall, Colleen raised her cigarette to her lips and held it there, not inhaling.

This is getting easy, Royce thought. He played the tension for a moment, then two, then said, "Same as always. He'd probably just love a night on the town with you, Eddie."

Eddie raised an eyebrow and nodded thoughtfully at his cigarette.

"But what he really wanted was to spend a lifetime giving Bobby whatever he wanted. He called Bobby Snowball, after some screwy novel he'd read, and would get his lines crossed in the office just making up stories about himself and Snowball."

Royce saw a plume of smoke bloom in the hallway in front of Colleen. Eddie continued to nod thoughtfully, his lips pursed, watching the smoke rise between his fingers.

"Bobby never had much to do with the queens, though. He liked the punks, I guess."

Eddie looked up.

"They call you Doc? That what they call you inside?" Colleen leaned around the corner and looked at Royce.

Royce nodded. He'd already told his name but Eddie wanted a handle. Several very dumb pseudonyms flashed across his mind. Lonnie Childs. Miles Torn. Elmer Ship-ault. But he was new at this undercover stuff. Besides, he had a driver's license and a truck registration and too many other ways to accidentally blow holes in his story to be fooling around with a fake name. So he told the truth. "Lots of them call me Doc, yeah. But the real name's Royce. Franklin Royce. Most folks call me Royce, or Frank." He shook his head and almost blushed. "Bobby called me Rolls. Rolls Royce." He smiled up at his two hosts. "Just like you, Eddie."

Eddie looked down at him. A ring of smoke spun away from the wall where Colleen stood.

For a moment all Royce could hear was a very loud silence. Then he noticed that the crickets in this part of Dallas were almost as loud as the ones outside the prison in Hunts-ville or his house in Giddings. Somewhere up the street beyond the mouth of the dead-end alley, someone leaned on a car horn and yelled something unintelligible. Some kind of whistle blew far away, tentatively. The heat was still with them. The exertion Eddie had just put himself through showed in the rivulets of sweat on his thin, muscular frame. Royce himself had a drop of sweat on the end of his nose, and his eyes stung from the salty moisture leaking into them from above. The small living room reeked of damp cigarette ashes and stale tobacco smoke and fried electronics and mildew and decay. The whistle got loud and turned out to be the persistent boil of water in a teakettle in the kitchen. Colleen Valdez' robe disappeared and soon the smell of cheap instant coffee found its way down the hall to the trashed living room, like the odor of fresh dirt dug from a trench.

Eddie flipped his cigarette through the hole in the front of the television set and hefted the hulk to his shoulder. He carried the ruined appliance out the front door, turned left onto the breezeway and dropped it over the banister at the back staircase. The television exploded on the pavement in the alley three stories below. When he came back in the apartment, Colleen had brought three cups of steaming bad coffee into the living room and offered one to Royce. There was no milk or sugar. The brew was rank and hot.

Sitting with his back against the wall, Royce found his attention once again drawn to Colleen's strange beauty. Her legs folded over the couch to the floor. The front of the robe slit over them to her thighs. These parts of her were perfectly beautiful, to Royce's thinking, and all the more fascinating when contrasted with her ruined yet haunting face. The beauty of her face hovered just beneath its devastated surface in the same way a fine design can be detected in the architecture of a house long since abandoned to the slow decay of the seasons. This is not to say that she was old by any means; she couldn't have been thirty. Aside from her face, and despite her apparent long career of dissolution, Colleen Valdez' body and figure had the suppleness and resilience of that of a seventeen-year-old girl. These assets were visible to Royce, and he felt urges and desires stirring that he'd denied himself for a long, long time. And he felt old and shapeless and unattractive as well.

Eddie and Colleen were making small talk about an upper-crust address. Royce paid little attention to them, finding himself instead drifting lazily on a wave of sensuality that lulled the aches so recently induced by Mr. Lamark, mixed strangely with them, assuaged their pain for him. He sat on the floor with his back to the wall, sipping hot coffee, not two feet from Colleen's calves and thighs. He tried to imagine how her skin might feel to his fingertips as they made their ways gingerly up her calves, over the rounded, dimpled knees, separating them gently, along the velvety unshaven insides of her thighs .

"Hey, Rolls Royce!" Eddie was addressing him. Royce tore his eyes off the fleshly mantra and found both Colleen and Eddie looking down at him from the sofa.

"Yo," Royce smiled sheepishly

"You still got that pickup truck?"

"At your service," he said gallantly. "Mind if I spend the night?"

"Not at all," Eddie said. "Any friend of Bobby Mink's is a friend of ours. We have a little job to do first, though. "

"Oh?" Royce looked from one face to the other and back.

"What's that?"

"Well," said Eddie simply, staring at Royce, "we still need to get a bottle of whiskey and television."

"Oh."

"That's why we thought we'd borrow your truck."

A slightly uncomfortable feeling was trying to make its way into Royce's brain, but he ignored it and said simply, "Sure. Borrow the truck. "

"Well," Eddie said, "you come with the truck, don't you? I mean," he opened his hands and closed them, one over the other, "you want to be at the wheel of your own truck, don't you?"

Attention, Royce thought, this is a test. "Sure. I guess. Do I? "

Colleen laughed. She had lovely teeth, though they were a little yellow from tobacco. Royce smiled. He could clean them for her.

"Sure you do," Eddie said. "Besides, you could wait in it if we need to, uh, double park or something."

"Right," Royce agreed, with a distant smile, "double park."

"Good," Eddie said. He slid open a drawer in the edge of the low table in front of them and pulled out a pistol.

The pit of Royce's stomach opened into a void. "What's—" he began, and his voice caught in his throat. The only thought in his head was that Lamark and Valdez had seen right through him, and now all they would he needing to know was where he'd parked his truck, and could they have the keys, please, before they took him out into armadillo country and blew him away.

Eddie stood up and smiled. The gun looked to be a .25 or .32 automatic. Not too big, but not particularly small, it was mostly black and very efficient looking. Eddie pulled back the slide until a slug nicked into the breach in front of it, then released the slide with a snap. Though he was undoubtedly trying to tell Royce something, Lamark made a point of keeping the muzzle of the gun pointed away from the populated areas of the room. He even snapped the safety on. He stuffed the business end of the gun down the front of his pants and went into the bedroom. "You use much, Doc?" he said from in there.

Royce cleared his throat and found his voice. "Use much," he repeated tonelessly.

"Yeah." Eddie came back through the door of the bedroom pulling on a longsleeved shirt and stood above him. The shirt had large yellow and purple flowers on it against a cream background, cut cowboy style. A double yoke in front dipped into breast pockets, each with a flap that closed with a pearl snap. Each long cuff closed snugly with three similar pearl snaps, but Eddie Lamark left these open and rolled them back a turn. He left two similar snaps open below his throat, exposing the upper rays of the torch of liberty tattooed on his chest, and buttoned the rest down the front of the shirt. He didn't tuck in the shirttails. When he was finished he looked casual in a loud and cheap sort of way. There was no sign of the gun beneath the flowers.

"Yeah," he said. "Use much dope?"

Royce looked from Colleen up to Eddie and said nothing.

"Sure you do," Lamark said, answering his own question. "A fancy doctor has to have a good reason to write scrips for dopers, rich or not, a kind of empathy, the kind that comes from mutual understanding of a mutual need."

Royce shook his head. "Quality pharmaceuticals are too hard to find in the joint," he said. "I'm clean." Colleen stood up from the sofa and went toward the bedroom. As she squeezed between Eddie and Royce in the doorway, Eddie rounded her behind with his hand and pinched the thin fabric that covered it. The material slid off her shoulders as she passed and left behind a glimpse of her nakedness as she entered the bedroom. Royce's eyes tore at this vision like caged ferrets. He sniffed the air as she passed. Eddie stood smiling in the doorway, leering at Royce, the robe dangling from his fingers. Royce wondered if Eddie could manage to understand the need he was beginning to feel for Eddie's girl. Maybe Eddie would like to prescribe Royce a little time with her.

As if reading Royce's thought, Eddie tossed the gown into the dark bedroom and said, "You up a long time?"

Royce hauled himself to his feet and brushed his stained khakis. "Two years and some."

"Suit you?"

"How's that? "Royce peered at him. Eddie had a quizzical, amused expression in his eyes.

"The life there suit you. No women and all that. "

Royce shook his head. "Worst part, I guess."

Eddie pursed his lips. "I guess Bobby adapted."

Royce had to think about that one for a moment. He remembered how Mencken had raised his pelvis off the stainless steel table as the morphine had gone in. A joke. It meant nothing in particular. Or had it?

Rather than hazard a guess, he passed on it. "I never did."

Eddie turned his head and scratched a sideburn. "Seems like a logical thing to do when you're in there long enough," he said. "Kinda make yourself at home."

Royce looked at him, astonished. "You've never been in the big house?"

Eddie looked at him and grinned.

"Nice going," Royce admitted. "How in hell have you managed that?"

Eddie just kept grinning. Like hell he'd never been in a joint.

Colleen appeared in the bedroom door. She had braided her

hair to look much shorter. She wore tennis shoes, jeans, a checked western shirt and hoop earrings. Only the first button above the high waist of the jeans was buttoned on the shirt. The V that widened up to her shoulders showed plenty of breast to Royce, more than he'd seen in a long time.

She patted Royce's belly. He could smell her hair, cigarettes and baby shampoo; the top of her head came to just below his nose. "How's the gut, Doc?" She had bright green eyes.

Royce bit his lip and tried to make a joke. "I can't tell if it's post-reptilian trauma or pre-caper butterflies. I mean," he looked from Lamark to Valdez and back, "are we going out to *buy* a television and a bottle of whiskey?"

Eddie ducked his head and scratched a sideburn. "That all depends," he said.

Colleen Valdez slapped her buttocks with both her hands and pushed her tightly denimed pelvis forward. "Let's ride," she said.

· TEN ·

The truck was where he'd left it. It was a Chevy Silverado, designed to haul a horse trailer, about five years old. Except for the damage recently applied to the front end by Pamela Royce, and the dust of Texas, the truck was a relatively clean one. A garage nearby Huntsville had repaired the headlights while Royce sat in a cafe and read the Mencken file, two days before.

Eddie looked at the front end and asked whether all the lights still worked. When Royce said they did, Eddie patted the hood with approval. "Nice truck."

Colleen sat in the middle and fiddled with the radio. In a moment she had found an all-night country music program on WBAP, aimed at truckers, and sat back contentedly, her arms stretched over the back of the seat behind her two companions. Royce drove.

First they bought a tank of gasoline so as to get a free trip through an automatic carwash.

"Now we're invisible," Eddie said. Then he navigated them to a street in University Heights where, he assured them, the residents were unlikely to have block security.

Royce was nervous. The first and last thing he'd ever stolen had been a watermelon when he was in junior high school, and he'd gotten caught. Slipping through the hot shadows of suburban Dallas looking for an easy score with two characters as desperate as he was scared, he seriously doubted the efficacy of his odyssey to vindicate Bobby Mencken's wrongful death. Even the terms seemed overblown. One look at Eddie showed him a sociopath capable of anything, who by luck and cunning had miraculously avoided any serious scrapes with the law, a man entirely despicable enough to have allowed Bobby Mencken to die for something he himself had done.

But why risk his life, as Royce was clearly doing, for a dead man he'd never known? To justify a squandered career, a medical practice so decrepit that he'd had to take on the odious millstone of being medical practitioner to several thousand miserable, desperate men in the Huntsville prison? To justify the actions of a financially cornered moonlighter who, masquerading behind the Hippocratic oath, had taken the job of ensuring humane conditions during state executions; and all because he couldn't control his own drinking or his wife's excessive and compulsive expenditures?

Or was it deeper than that? After so many years he wondered if life held anything more profound than monthly payments, overdrafts at the bank, unfair speeding tickets, a credit card scissored in two on a silver tray in a very nice restaurant, a life whose pecuniary rhythms sailed from troughs of embarrassment to peaks of anxiety and back again with no respite.

Which is the bigger waste? A man born with a chance who blows it, or a man born with no chance who fights it? They're both losers in the end, aren't they?

Yes and no, he decided. Bobby Mencken's death had shown him a true wrong dealt a man whose life, on its own level, had probably been no more or less screwed up than Royce's. Had such an injustice been perpetrated on Royce instead of Mencken, Royce would have fought tooth and nail for what he perceived as his God-given right to be allowed to continue his trivial suffering, rather than go through the twisted fate of being condemned to die for an act he hadn't committed.

Wouldn't he?

God-given indeed. Who was he kidding? You dance with your fate, or your fate dances with you. And nobody knows his fate until he's looking at it, until it's too late, until it's practically over.

God my ass. If Royce had taken a couple fewer drinks back when he was married to a rich cow man's beautiful daughter, and paid more attention to his lucrative practice in Corpus Christi, his whole life would have been different. If Bobby Mencken hadn't been jogging past a convenience store and found a gun on the sidewalk, just after somebody inside had been shooting the proprietor, as he'd claimed at his trial, the verdict might have been different. His life might have been allowed to go on. If he'd been a white man his whole life would have been different. As it was, the jury had laughed when the prosecutor summed up Mencken's testimony.

He recalled an old Huntsville con who used to quote a ditty as Royce dressed the man's persistently gangrenous leg.

> Life is a game of poker.
> Happiness is in the pot.
> You're dealt five cards from the cradle,
> And you play them whether you like it or not.

Royce smiled bitterly. This is a Darwinian precept. The pair of deuces and your good looks are your inherited traits. The aces and queens across the table are your environment. Much later, it had turned out that the gangrene had persisted for so long because the con wanted it that way. He was using the cavity of the wound and its bandage to smuggle contraband goods around the prison, mostly drugs and weapons. The cache might never have been discovered had he not lost consciousness in the sweltering yard one day and been delivered to the infirmary. In the leg beneath the dressing they found 150 sodium amytal capsules. Royce was forced to amputate the leg before a decent surgeon could be gotten from Houston to Huntsville. Three days later the man died anyway. Just before he lost consciousness for the last time, he half opened his eyes and recognized Royce at the foot of his bed. He winked and said, "Life is just a game of poker...."

"Einstein said something about God and dice," the old con said to him once. "But God doesn't use dice. He runs a poker game. There's a difference."

God my ass, Royce thought.

Justice, even retroactive justice, seemed a clear alternative to that final outrage. And in the act of securing justice for Bobby Mencken, Royce thought he could see a way to secure a modicum of dignity for his own miserable life— justification, even.

But there was more to it than that. More than justice. More than justification. More than dignity. Nothing less than, perhaps, revenge.

Revenge for whom? For Mencken?

Mencken didn't need any avenging, he was beyond it. Technically, morally, that's what Royce was up to. But, as they say in Pravda sometimes, Royce was technically and morally worn out. What he wanted was revenge for the miserable, vacuous betrayal his own life had become.

Go home? No. No more home.

At a stop sign beneath a streetlight, Royce fingered the two burns throbbing on his neck above his left shoulder. Besides, enough was enough. He had a score to settle with this Eddie Lamark.

As they approached a streetlight and drew under and away from it, Colleen Valdez touched the double burn with her fingertips. A thrill Royce hadn't known in years traversed the length of his spine.

"Slow down," said Eddie tersely, turning down the radio. Royce did so. They idled past a large, dark house. No cars were visible in the driveway; no windows were lit. A lawn looking dark gray in the obscurity stretched from the street between the driveway on the right and a row of large, drooping willow trees on the left. Royce tried to see the place through the eyes of Eddie Lamark, as a set-up for a heist. The trees provided a perfect avenue of approach, beneath which an intruder would be well concealed from both the house and the street. All the windows on the first story were double hung, and potentially of easy access. The house was big and old and moderately prosperous, and therefore likely to contain many glitzy portable consumer items, suitable for quick resale. Most important, it looked as if nobody was home. Most important for the occupants, that is. Eddie wouldn't care one way or the other. Eddie would like a nice straight-ahead job, but on the other hand, he would love trouble.

There was always the chance that the house might contain a feisty old grandmother, who came west with Roy Bean and would settle Eddie's hash with the sawed-off ten-gauge she kept under the bed. That would leave Colleen and Royce sitting in the pickup truck, slightly shocked at the loud discharge that woke the neighborhood and the flash that momentarily lit up one of the upper story windows.

Leaning over Colleen to case the house with the others, Royce dropped his eye to Colleen's cleavage and thought about that eventuality, how nice it could be if Eddie would just disappear. After a moment he looked up in the darkness. He could see the whites of her large eyes, slightly wider than they were high, looking down at him.

Eddie sat back against the seat and stared ahead. "Watch where you're going," he hissed. Royce quickly looked forward and jerked the steering wheel. The pickup had drifted to the right and narrowly missed colliding with the rear end of a very new looking Lincoln parked half on the grass strip that ran along the side of the tree-lined street. The pickup's front wheels squealed a little as he corrected their direction.

Eddie was all business. He said nothing about Royce's indiscretion, but sat rigidly in the darkness, thinking.

"Thirty minutes," he said. "There a clock in this thing?"

Royce pushed a button on the radio and the correct time replaced the frequency of the country station in a liquid crystal display on the dash, black letters against a cool green: 11:25 P.M.

"Thirty-five minutes. Drop me at the corner," Eddie said. He ran the flat of his hand back and forth over the door. "How do you get out of this fucking thing?"

"Under the armrest."

Eddie found the latch and put his hand on it. "You see those trees on the left?"

"Willows," Royce said.

"Thirty-five minutes from now, midnight. You drive slow from the other end of the block; you don't change speed much. Don't come all the way down this same street. Zigzag onto it at the other end of the block, maybe two blocks away. But not too slow. No radio. I'll be in the willows and see you coming. Flick your brights twice. Let Colleen hold this door off the latch. If I come out with much stuff you'll have to stop. Otherwise keep going real slow. I'll hop in. If I don't show, ease out of here and don't come back." He gently worked the latch and opened the door a few inches. A loud, highly fractious, whining buzz that sounded like the back-up warning on a cement truck began to pulsate on the dash, and a woman's voice said, "Your passenger door is ajar. Please close your passenger door. Your passenger door is ajar. Please close—"

"Jesus Christ, what is that?" Eddie said. He pulled the door to the jamb and the tone stopped. "Turn the corner."

Royce took a right.

"Fix that thing before you come back," Eddie hissed, then he went out the door. Colleen neatly caught the armrest and closed the door with a click. The dash alarm whined but didn't have time to say its piece. Royce gradually accelerated to the next corner and took a left, checking the rear-view mirror as he turned. In spite of the loud shirt there was no sign of Lamark.

They drove in silence for a moment, Royce concentrating on every detail he could make out by the headlights.

"I assume you know where we are," he said after a few more turns, "because I'm completely lost."

Colleen reopened the door and slammed it. "Keep going straight," she said. They rode in silence for a few minutes, both watching the street in front of them. The suburban area began to open into a more commercial one. The street became four lanes with a divider in the middle. Soon business enterprises, most of them closed for the night, sprung up on both sides of the thoroughfare. "Turn here," she said suddenly. Royce did so. His headlights were swallowed by an intensely illuminated area displaying four rows of shiny cars and trucks. Behind them a high white facade read: LANEY AND SONS, USED CARS AND TRUCKS in tall red capital letters. She pointed. "Drive to the left and then turn away from the street between the buildings." Royce did so. The next building over was completely dark, set away from the used car lot by a narrow dirt alley. Swerving over the dirt the headlights showed a sign above two tall roll-away doors on the front of the dark building: LANEY'S LIVERY STABLE, HORSES AND TRAILERS, BLACKSMITH. "Behind the livery," she said. Royce drove between the two buildings and found his way blocked by a maze of fenced corrals, small sheds with corrugated tin roofs, gates, loading chutes and odd vehicles. Here and there the eye of a horse glinted in the beams of his headlights. A row of horse trailers of every age and description blocked their way on the left. He backed across the access so that the truck was heading more or less out and switched off the motor and lights. Behind them a dark mound loomed as high as the top of the tailgate. The odor of horse manure was very strong.

"Nice," Royce said. "If anybody comes looking for us we can just put a For Sale sign on the truck and burrow into the horse shit. Nobody'll ever find us."

"What time is it?"

Royce turned the key and fingered the button on the dash: 12:42. "That was quick."

"Can you fix that dingus?"

"What? You mean the Your Door Is Ajar dingus? Are you serious?"

She looked at him in the darkness.

"Shit," Royce said. "There's a pair of pliers, I mean," he caught himself, "three years ago there were tools in the dash there," he said, pointing at the dash pocket. "See if they're still there."

She opened the glove box. The light that flooded out of it lit her face and gave it a very mysterious look, with her black hair partially obscuring it, like a sandblasted Madonna, as she leaned to sort through the junk in the glove compartment.

Royce switched the ignition key on, without starting the engine, and wedged himself upside down under the dashboard beneath the steering wheel. To do so he had to stick one foot out the open window to Colleen's right, and fold the other up against the seat to her left. She worked over and under his left leg as she searched for tools in the glove compartment.

"Flashlight?" he asked. "Lighter?"

"There's a penlight."

"Perfect," Royce said glumly. His head was wedged between the brake and gas pedals. He had to keep a strain on his neck and shoulder muscles to prevent gouging the back of his head on the corners of the pedals, his shoulders against the floormat. Working by the odd patches of light that leaked backward from the dash, he wedged one hand into the mass of wires and linkages above the steering column and found a small enclosed chassis that he thought might contain the terminals for the various standard and optional signaling devices on the truck. Holding it with one hand he worked his other hand through a loop in a heater hose and found the tabs for the cover. "Turn the light on and hand it to me," he said. "Put it in my mouth."

She had to lean over the middle of his upturned torso to do this, so that her breasts lay against his abdomen. Royce, concentrating on the maze in the darkness over his head, would not have felt a more electrifying jolt shoot through him if he had shorted out the entire truck. He inhaled sharply between clenched teeth. Suddenly he was seventeen years old again.

Colleen felt this charge run through him and laughed gently in the darkness. In spite of her proximity to him, she could not see Royce's mouth beneath the steering column, so she felt for it with her fingers. Then she passed the thin tube of the penlight between his lips and teeth. Then she pulled it out a little. Then she put it back in a little. At the same time she gently flattened her breasts against Royce's chest. He could distinctly feel one firm nipple against his lower rib.

"I like a man with a truck," she said.

"I got it, I got it," he said around the penlight, and gripped it with his teeth. Her fingernails caressed his cheek and disappeared out of the thin beam of the flash and back under the dash.

Boy, thought Royce, maneuvering the light up onto the wires above his face, never a dull moment with this bunch.

But then her hands found the zipper to his khaki pants and flattened the length of it against the very essence of his memory of youth, just as he got the top off the plastic box.

"12:49," she said, and she pulled the tab of the zipper. Royce could feel every tooth on the zipper as the tab separated them. "You think you can get finished before I do?"

Ye gods and little fishes, Royce thought. "What about Eddie?" he said around the body of the penlight.

"Better hurry up," she said playfully, "or we'll blow everything."

My God, Royce thought with a strange sense of urgency, this woman knows everything about me. "Open the side door," he hissed. His breath was coming quickly, and because of the penlight most of it came through his nose, bringing with it the powerfully combined odors of horse manure and vinyl. No woman had willingly touched him in more years than he cared to remember.

Without interrupting what she had begun, Colleen freed one hand and cracked the side door. The annoying buzzer sounded, and the synthetic woman's voice repeated its warning message.

"Your passenger door is ajar. Please close your passenger door. Your passenger door is ajar...."

Royce could barely think as he methodically unplugged and re-plugged wires from the terminal strip inside the plastic chassis. His neck was in an uncomfortable strain, but now he willingly thrust his shoulders against the floormat as she took him in her mouth and worked him with her hand.

"...passenger door," the voice continued. It had been pro-grammed to nag seductively. But Royce and Colleen quickly discov-ered a use for its rhythm. "Your passenger door is ajar. Please close your passenger door. Your passenger door is ajar. Please close your passenger door... ."

The fifth wire silenced the alarm, and for a moment the only sounds to be heard in the truck were those usually associated with gluttony, backed up by the incessant whirr of all the crickets in Texas. Somewhere in the darkness a horse whinnied contentedly. Royce's face was running with perspiration; it left a wet streak on the floormat as he turned it aside and spit the penlight against the truck door. He moaned deeply, loudly and thoroughly, in the throes of a pleasure he hadn't experienced in a long, long time. It was enough to make him weep. Tears in fact started to his eyes and he kicked the foot dangling out the passenger window so high the window frame banged his shin. His spasm lasted longer than he'd ever known or thought possible.

Hardly had his shudders reduced to a mild trembling when Colleen kissed him and zipped him up.

"You won," she said. "Let's ride." She slid out of the truck, opening the door so that Royce's leg fell onto the seat. Royce quickly replaced the plastic cover over the terminal strip and struggled out from under the dash. Colleen got back in the truck as he started it. He accelerated back out of the dirt drive between the livery stable and the parking lot. She slammed the glove box closed and pointed up the road.

"You're right, baby," Royce said huskily, and rubbed her thigh. "I won." He was breathing as heavily as if he'd just run from the fifty-yard line to the press box in the Cotton Bowl. But he felt like a new man. "You know what you just did for me?" he began effusively. "You just—" He caught himself. He just barely caught himself. Another moment, she would have had it all. Pamela, the overpriced ranch they couldn't afford, the top-of-the-line Mercedes, the country club, all of it, right down to the last time he and Pamela had made love, badly, in '74 or '75 it might have been, right down to the fact that he'd never known Bobby Mencken at all, much less done hard time. But after a silence he said softly, "Two and a half years in stir. And I'm straight."

He looked at the woman on the seat beside him. The shadows of the streetlights slipped over her shape in the darkness. "Take a right," she said, her right hand holding onto the doorframe and her left onto the dash. "Now a left."

"Colleen, why?" he asked, driving quickly, watching where they were going. "Why me?"

"Hey," she said simply, "you're helping me; I'll help you."

Oh boy, Royce thought, the primitive barter system.

"Besides," she smiled, "crime turns me on."

Royce held his breath a moment, then let a long, low, almost inaudible whistle escape his pursed lips. He had washed up among a fast crowd.

She glanced nervously at the dash. "What time is it?" she demanded, pointing at it.

"Take it easy," Royce said. "That's a radio station. Here." He pushed the proper button and the time replaced the frequency: 12:02.

"We're late," she said between clenched teeth. "Right at the next corner; there's a hydrant. Get our ass to the next cross street and slow down in the block after that."

Royce threw the truck around the corner. The outside wheels squealed on the black tarmac and he had already depressed the accelerator before he saw that the next block was filled with flashing red and blue lights.

"Cops!" she hissed. "Goddamn it!"

Royce's blood turned cold. He couldn't think. He had the sense to back off on the accelerator immediately without slamming on the brakes. He tapped them enough to slow the truck down before they got to the last cross street, a block before the house with the willow trees.

"Don't turn!"

Colleen slammed the dash with her fist and slid over the seat until she was as close to Royce as she could get.

"Turn on that goddamn radio," she said quickly, watching the street. "Never mind. I'll get it. Keep driving straight."

"Are you crazy?" Royce said.

"Do just like we're supposed to!" She fiddled with the dials without taking her eyes off the street in front of them. In a moment the languid strains of a banal country tune filled the cab of the truck: "... *and you decorated my life...*"

Colleen sat back and put her arm over his shoulders. "We're rubbernecking," she said.

He did as he was told. They really had little choice. In the next block three police cars were parked at various angles in the street in front of the house with the willow trees. Each had its headlights on and its roof lights flashing. Dark figures moved among the swiveling beams of red and blue. As Royce and Colleen drove past the intersection they saw a cop lighting the flares that would soon prevent access to the next block. The cop looked at them.

"We should turn—" Royce began.

"Keep going," she said evenly, as she watched the officer with the frank curiosity of those born innocent and destined to die the same way. Flickering crimsons and the odor of burning magnesium wafted through the cab as they passed, and they could hear the flares spitting on the asphalt.

Royce slowed the truck to a crawl as he threaded his way through the cars and policemen in the street. The big house set back off the street by its driveway and willow trees was completely illuminated, and uniformed figures moved about in front of it. An ambulance was parked sideways on the lawn, its doors open. A spotlight showed a low stretcher on wheels, its sheets thrown back and straps dangling from it. The front doors of the house and the garage were wide open. People milled about on the steps and in the entry hall beyond. The garage and every window had lights in them.

Not a chance, Royce thought to himself, not a chance for Eddie. A sudden pang of sympathy arose in him for Lamark. As they slowly passed the house Colleen slid over to the passenger door. She leaned out of the window as if to get a last glance of a sensational scene in a quiet neighborhood, but Royce heard the click of the door latch under the armrest.

"What the hell are you doing?" he growled. But just then, as they drove past the Lincoln, parked right where it had been before, a cop came into the headlights. He stood on the side of the road in front of the nearest willow tree, almost exactly where Eddie had said he'd wait. The cop pointed away from them, down the street, with a flashlight in his right hand, and waved them on with a circular motion of his left.

"Hi, officer," Colleen said brightly, as the cop moved past the passenger window. "What's going on?" She sounded exactly like a dumb teenager. She even pretended to chew gum as she talked.

"Move along, please," the cop said impatiently, looking up the road in the direction he wanted them to go.

"Gee," Colleen said, and sat back in the seat just as the passenger window moved past the cop. She lowered her voice. "Ready to go road racing? Turn the corner," she said matter-of-factly, staring expectantly ahead. In her hands she held the armrest and window handle of the passenger door.

His heart pounding in his chest, Royce did as he was told. He turned right, around the hedge that hid the last house on the block.

A police car was parked there, on the opposite side of the street. Two uniformed officers were getting flares out of its open trunk.

There was no sign of Eddie.

Colleen bit her lip. "'Et's get out of here," she said dully. Royce made a left at the next corner, much as they had done the last time. Then he took a right, then a left, then another right.

After a while Colleen opened the passenger door wide and slammed it hard.

· ELEVEN ·

A few minutes after they left the scene of the crime, Royce asked a very simple question.

"Where to?"

Colleen Valdez scowled. "Fuck off!"

"Oh."

He found the Northwest Highway and got on it going west. Then he drove north for a little while on Harry Hines Boulevard. When they came to the Lyndon Johnson Freeway he got on that heading east. After a while the LBJ goes south and he followed it. If they stayed on it long enough, they would circle the entire city.

After a half-hour or so it seemed she was going to let them do just that. Colleen Valdez sat as far away from Royce as possible and brooded against the glass in the passenger door.

Soon they were on the south end of Dallas, opposite the side of the city they'd started from. A sign warned of the impending intersection with the Thorton Freeway. She spoke.

"You got any money?"

Royce watched the highway.

She slid across the seat and placed one hand on the back of his neck and the other between his legs. The movement was so sudden Royce jumped in his seat and changed half a lane.

After a couple minutes of silence she asked him nicely, "You got any money, Frank?"

Royce shrugged against her persuading hands. "I got a few bucks."

"Thirty?"

He looked at her. "Sure."

She gave him a fond squeeze. "Take the Thorton, Highway 35."

They took it north and got off going west on Illinois Avenue.

A few blocks past Zang Boulevard they turned south, then back east, then south…. He knew they were near her apartment but it wasn't exactly the same neighborhood. That is to say, it was the same kind of neighborhood, run down, lots happening on the streets in spite of the hour— perhaps because of it—but not the exact same one. She pointed. "Here." He parked the truck across the street from an all-night grocery. Several people were leaning against the fenders of the cars out front, hanging around. "Let's see the thirty," she said.

Royce pulled out two twenties and gave them to her.

"Can you fit some whiskey into that?" he asked hopefully. "Ezra Brooks?"

She got out of the truck without answering.

He watched her cross the street. She had a fine body, seen from behind. Or from the front, for that matter. Were there other people like her in the world, who took sex so casually?

Instead of going into the grocery, she rounded the corner and disappeared into the darkness. The men and women hanging around the corner paid her little notice.

Half an hour passed.

Royce jerked awake when he heard the truck door open. She slid into the passenger seat and slammed the door.

"'Es go," she said in a thick voice.

He started the truck and pulled onto the street.

"Where?"

She didn't answer him. A package thumped to the floorboard at her feet. She'd fallen asleep against the doorjamb.

"Hey," he said a little more loudly, "where we going?"

She didn't answer. He pulled over to the curb and stopped.

"Hey, Colleen." He shook her.

"Home." She smacked her lips like a sleeping baby. Then she looked at him in a most peculiar manner, by leaning her head back as far to one side as it would go and peering at him from beneath eyelids seriously under the influence of gravity. In spite of the gloom, each pupil was tiny, in about the same proportion to the rest of the eye as a ladybug to an eight ball. She didn't look so pretty like that.

"S'long Eddie...."

Then her eyelids gave up their resistance and closed.

Royce retrieved the package from the floor between her feet. It was a brown paper bag and it contained two packs of Salems, matches, and a pint of Old Overholt. The seal on the bottle hadn't been broken.

"Forty bucks," he muttered, and cracked the seal.

The whiskey was decent. As it corroded its way to his stomach he realized how much tension he'd built up. After another hit on the bottle he decided crime wasn't his bag. Too much pressure. His career as wheel man was showing a hundred percent failure rate.

On the other hand...

He contemplated the woman nodding a foot or two away from him. On the other hand, if Eddie Lamark had really blown it and gotten himself nailed red-handed breaking and entering, Frank Royce had inherited a right nice little spread. He took a third swallow. A man could get used to that idea.

He took a fourth, smaller swallow. No way Eddie and Colleen and Royce combined could make bail, no way conceivable. Pity. A slow grin crept over his unshaven face.

A little time passed. He idly tapped the neck of the bottle between his legs with a fingernail and watched the traffic. Big trucks ground past him, moving into the nighttime city to drop their loads. He heard laughter, a radio, a bottle break on the sidewalk. Behind all that he could hear a train. A silent white Cadillac limousine with a pair of steer horns bolted to its hood slowed as it glided down the opposite side of the street, made a U-turn in front of the grocery and eased into the parking space he'd left a few minutes before. He watched it in the side mirror of the truck. Colleen made little smacking sounds with her lips and twisted listlessly into the corner between the seat and armrest. The wide front door of the Cadillac opened into the street and a chauffeur in immaculate powder-blue livery cut like a western leisure suit stepped out. He flattened his string tie against his chest as he looked both ways, then crossed the street and disappeared around the same corner as Colleen had. None of the five or six people hanging around on the corner paid him any mind either.

Nice business, Royce thought. He sipped his pint, and idly speculated on just what kind of ostentation it would take to get a little attention in this neighborhood.

After awhile Colleen stirred and opened her eyes halfway.

"Where are we?"

"I was going to ask you that."

She laughed a breathy, quiet laugh. "Oh man," she said, "I'm so susceptible." She smacked her lips slowly. Once, twice.

Royce leered at her. "So now what?"

"Home," she said. "But first, let's make a little stop."

"Colleen," he sighed. "It's three-thirty in the morning."

"Just a short one," she said. "How's the booze?'

He held up the half-empty bottle. "Not Ezra, not bad. Want some?"

She shook her head, "I'm straight," and gave him directions.

He looked at his side mirror. "I always liked that term, "straight," for being high," he said as he pulled away from the curb.

She shrugged. "It's an upside-down world."

The next stop was only two blocks away.

"Wait here," she said when they'd parked.

They were in a very run-down neighborhood. Across the street was a storefront with radios and televisions in windows to each side of the door. In each window, one television was turned on and tuned to the same channel as the other. Expanded metal screen was nailed over both windows and the door.

When she returned she was lugging a small color television. She put it in the truck bed and got up front with Royce.

She had to wake him up. "You've been gone a half-hour," he said grumpily.

"Here's your money," she said, and thrust a handful of bills into his hand.

He looked at it stupidly.

"It's almost all there," she said defensively. "I had to pay for the pint."

"I, I…"

"I saved a little downtown for just the two of us, too." She smiled shyly. "We can chase it."

"Downtown?"

"Junk."

"Junk?"

"Yeah, *heroin*."

"Golly."

Royce looked dumbly at the pint between his legs, nearly empty now. Then he looked through the back window at the television.

"It's a Sony Trinitron," she said dully. "Better than the one we had." She looked at him. Her green eyes could not have been greener because their pupils could not have been smaller. Royce wondered if she knew who he was.

"We?" he asked archly.

"Yeah," she leered cutely. "We."

Royce shook his head.

He liked the sound of it. She was a junkie. He knew that. She'd probably just sold herself to one guy for the fix and to another guy for the television. There must have been some kind of snag about the whiskey and cigarettes, or she'd have worked out an arrangement over that, too.

Yet she'd said "We."

He liked the sound of it.

Need another bottle, he said to himself.

They finally made it home at a quarter after five.

She had him plug in the television. Then she made him salvage the mangled rabbit ears from the alley below the back stairs, where Eddie had flung them with the old television, and hook them up to the new one. Then she made him turn it on.

It was all on the early-bird news, right after the farm report still incongruously broadcast to the city of Dallas.

"Robbery and murder in exclusive University Park," the lead-in said, "right after this." Royce had almost fallen asleep in his chair with a fresh fifth of whisky in his lap. But he stiffened when he heard the announcer's voice and steeled himself to listen through the commercial, his eyes closed. The music and voices seemed obnoxiously loud and meaningless. The two and a half minutes of advertising between the lead-in and the story seemed endless. Finally the newscaster reappeared. Royce opened his eyes. The story logo appeared on the wall behind a well-groomed man seated in the television studio. It was the same guy he'd watched the other night in the bar, or could have been.

"Responding to reports of gunfire in the exclusive University Park district around midnight tonight, police discovered the body of Mrs. Tyler Greyson in the bedroom of her family home."

Overexposed footage from a hand-held camera appeared on the wall behind the newscaster, then filled the screen. The tape was a melange of whirling lights, police cars, faces, uniforms, and hands held up against the bright lights behind the camera. In the background appeared the mansion Royce had seen in University Park, and the row of willow trees leading up to it.

"Oh shit, Eddie, oh dear," Colleen said.

"A police spokeswoman said that Mrs. Greyson evidently had surprised an intruder in her home at around ten minutes to midnight, and shots were exchanged. A neighbor had this to say."

The footage cut to the brightly illuminated face of a man in a checked western shirt and dark glasses. He explained how he and his wife had heard the distinctive roar of Mrs. Greyson's .44, followed by the subsequent pops of a smaller caliber gun.

"Police arriving upon the scene within five minutes of the call received no response at Mrs. Greyson's front door. The garage door, however, was standing open, and Mrs. Greyson's car was missing. Upon further investigation, Mrs. Greyson was discovered seriously wounded on the upper landing of the front staircase. The police spokeswoman said she was dressed in a nightgown, and had been shot more than once at close range, in the face."

Royce became very alert, all ears and eyes now. The convenience store operator had been shot in the same way. He stole a look at Colleen. She was curled on the sofa, her eyes fastened to the television screen.

It was a cinch Bobby Mencken hadn't pulled the trigger on Mrs. Greyson, and Colleen hadn't either; she'd been with Royce, helping him work on his truck.

Eddie had pulled this one.

"An antique .44 Colt revolver," the newsman continued, "was discovered beneath her body, and the police spokeswoman said the weapon had been recently fired. Another policeman, however, said that the weapon could not possibly have been the one used to shoot Mrs. Greyson."

You're right, it wasn't the .44, Royce thought. The weapon used to shoot Mrs. Greyson would turn out to be a .25 or a .32 automatic, the same caliber that had killed the convenience store clerk.

The footage of the front of the house cut to a policeman, looking down under the brim of his hat at a microphone, who said, "No way. It's simple as that. One shot from a weapon of that caliber would have took her whole head off."

Another angle of the neighbor standing with his hands in his back pockets, shaking his head as an off-camera voice said, "Think she could have shot herself in the face accidentally?" "No way no way no way," the man rejoined decisively as the microphone was thrust back in his face. "She loved that old gun. She had it years and years and she knew how to use it and didn't have no reason to kill herself. Her grandchildren was all just here on Saturday." The footage cut to an ambulance parked approximately where Royce remembered seeing it, half on and half off the lawn in front of the house. Then the picture cut to the ambulance turning slowly out of the driveway. Royce chewed his lip. What the hell had Eddie gotten into? Had he blown away somebody's grandmother for a television set? Just like he'd blown away somebody's mother for a six-pack? But there was something else. If this Mrs. Greyson was dead, Colleen and Royce were accessories to murder.

"Mrs. Greyson was taken to Southern Methodist Hospital, where she was pronounced dead on arrival, at one-thirty-five this morning."

That's what I like about the electronic age, Royce thought, you always have up-to-the-minute information.

As the commentator turned over his sheet of paper, another was thrust in front of him. "This just in," he said, taking the paper and reading it. "Police officers responding to an all-points bulletin describing Mrs. Greyson's car have recovered that car in Highland Park, not far from the Greyson home. Acting on an earlier description given by a neighbor, who said he was walking his dog near the Greyson home when he saw a man in a highly colorful flowered shirt drive away in Mrs. Greyson's personal car at a high rate of speed, police now say they have a suspect in custody." The commentator looked up from the paper. "To repeat that, police now say that they have taken into custody a man suspected of shooting to death Mrs. Tyler Greyson in her own home earlier this morning." He set the new page aside. "We'll bring you more details on this sad incident as they develop.

"Now this."

An unconscionably irritating jingle burst over the airwaves into the close little room, and Royce turned it down. On the silent screen, jet airplanes took off and landed, rows of people smiled and ate food off trays, the names of cities aligned themselves with prices.

Neither of them spoke. After a short while Royce took a swallow of whiskey.

"Thing does give good color," he said. Colleen said nothing.

"Shot her in the face," he said thoughtfully.

Colleen's eyes flicked from watching the images on the screen to him and back again.

Royce looked at her. "Hey," he said. After a moment she looked at him. "How come Bobby Mencken took the rap for him?" He gestured toward the screen with the bottle but kept his eyes on her.

She stared at him for a moment, then looked down at the floor between them.

"Why? I don't get it. The guy's crazy. Shooting women in the face."

She chewed her lip and stared at nothing.

"There must have been a reason," Royce said, waving the bottle.

"Assuming he was innocent, that was a big fall to take. Hell, it was a big fall to take even if he was guilty."

Still she said nothing.

Royce leaned forward and placed a hand on her arm.

"Colleen," he said gently. "If that's Eddie they got with that car, we're never going to see him again."

She looked at the television, looked at him, then looked at the floor.

"He thought I did it," she said quietly.

Royce sat very still.

"Who did? Bobby?"

She looked at him. A tiny muscle shivered at the corner of her mouth. "Eddie let him think it. I couldn't do anything about it. He said he'd…"

"What? He said he'd what?"

Her green eyes were open wide now. Royce could see she was afraid. "Eddie and Bobby took me off the streets," she said. "No man would have me, except for… except for…"

Royce moved from his chair to sit beside her on the sofa. "What happened, Colleen," he said, taking her hand solicitously. "Tell me about it."

She looked earnestly into his eyes. "I'm good at it, aren't I, Royce? Aren't I?"

Royce felt a twinge in his groin as she said it. If only she knew, he thought. How couldn't she? I mean, she *knows*. "Yeah, baby," he said, patting her two hands between his own, "the best."

"Really?" she said, in a tiny voice.

"Honest. A man like me, in stir for, um… two and a half years, he develops certain standards." He smiled grimly. "What happened in that convenience store?" She glanced toward the television.

"Look," Royce said, "Eddie's a media star now. He won't frequent the same places he used to." He narrowed his eyes. "Will he squeal on us?"

She shrugged. "What's to squeal? Even if he did, I mean, unless somebody saw us, I mean, even if they did, we didn't kill anyone." She smiled halfheartedly. "At the time, we were having sex behind a livery stable five miles away."

Royce thought about that. Then he brightened. "Yeah," he said, "there'd be tire tracks in that dirt yard, maybe. But nothing to connect us to Eddie. Not unless you and he…"

She shook her head. "Never been in a scrape with the law since I met Eddie. I mean," she blushed, "we haven't been caught." Then she frowned. "Bobby Mink got caught though. Oh Royce," she sighed, "he was such a wonderful guy. I never met anybody like Bobby Mink…."

Her voice trailed off and she looked away.

"Yeah," Royce said quietly. "Me neither." He straightened up and fiddled with the cap to the whiskey bottle on the table.

"So it was Eddie killed that woman in the Won-Stop."

Still looking away from him, she bit her lip and nodded. "Bobby was outside looking out for us. Eddie and I were inside. Eddie had the gun. She—" Colleen shook her head and a tear rolled down her cheek, "she just looked at Eddie when he asked for the money, just looked at him." She sighed. "He had a gun in his hand, this ugly little black pistol." She looked at her hand. "Ugliest, meanest looking thing I ever saw. Looked like some kind of nasty insect from some place where there's no light, ever." She glanced at him and looked away. "I don't know. It was the same kind as he had with him to—" she looked at the television, "tonight…." She shuddered. "He likes that kind."

Royce offered her the bottle. She worried the inside of her elbow with the other hand and refused it.

"She said, 'Put that pea-shooter away, punk.' Just like that. 'Put that damn li'l ol' pea-shooter away, punk, and git the hell out of here.'

"Eddie said, 'You touched it, you stupid bitch. What in hell you go and do that for? Huh? What in hell you go and do that for!' He was crying. I didn't know what he was talking about at the time, but it turned out he meant she had tromped on the burglar-alarm switch under the counter with her foot while she was talking tough with us. 'You coulda just give us the money, old woman,' he said. 'Come on, you coulda just give us the goddamn money. Shit,' he said. 'Do it now!' That's when we first heard the sirens. You can't believe how fast they came. This woman behind the counter gave us this real mean grin; she was gloating, Frank; she was proud she had made this boy cry with a gun in his hand. 'You're all alike,' she said, 'and I'm sick to death of it.' And you know, Royce, I don't think he'd have shot her yet, but then she pulled the key out of the cash register, you know, the key that turns it on? I mean you can't even get into the thing unless that key's in it. And she flung it across the room, like this." Colleen flung her arm sideways toward the television, without turning loose of her elbow.

"I watched it sail across the room, Royce," she continued, staring at a picture in her mind. "It was the slowest thing you ever saw. It just floated over the canned goods, gleaming in the air under those bright lights like there was all the time in the world for it to get over to the ice cream. Sure, like it was shopping or something. You know, with all that slow music they play for you to shop in the supermarket with? It was like the key itself was making the siren noise, you know?" She paused and looked at Royce. Royce stared at her for a moment, then shook his head.

"I said, 'We better go, Eddie,'" her lower lip quivered, "and then he shot her," she said, in a funny voice. She pointed her finger, thumb up. "He just started screaming and emptied the gun into her face…."

· TWELVE ·

"I was standing right next to him, on the same side as the one the gun threw the shells out of. It was an automatic, right? You saw one tonight just like it. Eddie likes them. They're hot when they come of the gun, you know, the shells, with smoke coming out of them. They were hopping all over the side of my face and neck and arm, stinging me, like. I thought I was in a swarm of wasps or something. But I was too scared to move. I just jumped every time the gun went off right beside me, and then in between shots a shell would skitter over my shoulder and sting a little every place it touched, because they're so hot from just being fired.

"I screamed to Eddie to stop but all I could do was watch the bullets hit that lady's face. I remember the shells stinging me and bouncing off me into the rows of potato chips in the stand in front of the counter and onto the floor. They were rolling around all over the place; it sounded like somebody had thrown a pocket full of change or... It was like I didn't really hear the shots.

"And then Eddie grabbed me and ran toward the back of the store. There was a window back there behind the walk-in cooler with a fan going in it. Eddie tore the fan loose with one hand and pushed me through headfirst. I landed in a pile in the dirt out behind the store, and then Bobby was there, yelling like, except he was whispering. 'What'd you do, what'd you do?' He kept saying it over and over again until Eddie pitched him the pistol out the window and yelled 'She shot her! Split!' Bobby Mink just backed up and stood there and looked at the hot gun in his hands and then looked at Eddie. I said 'What? Eddie...' 'Go on, run!' Eddie yelled. 'Get away from here and get rid of it! We'll meet you home!'"

She was crying now; her tears trickled over her ruined face to the corners of her mouth twisted by the memory. "I had about one second to say different and I didn't. I let Bobby believe it, and then he was gone." She looked at Royce. "I mean, it didn't make any difference; we still had to get rid of the gun...." She looked away. After a moment she shook her head. "He ran. It was as simple as that. He turned the corner... and... He turned the corner, and was... gone...."

She chewed her lip and made a conscious effort to stop her head from shaking side to side.

"Eddie was always the smartest in a situation like that. He always knew what to do and would do it way before anybody else knew what he was thinking about. It was a long time..." She inhaled deeply, her breath shivering as it went in, and sighed. "He isn't called 'Fast' for nothing...." She began to cry. Royce pulled a large blue calico neckerchief out of his back pocket and offered it to her.

"Thanks," she said simply, She blew her nose.

"It was a long time before I realized that he was as ahead of that situation that night as anyone could have been. He came out the window finally. I was still laying on the ground. He grabbed my arm and pulled me up without a word. About that time the sirens got their loudest, and we heard somebody lock up their brakes and slide to a stop, and the siren died, and there was a bang, not like a shot, but like somebody had jumped on a car hood or something, and the loudest, most out-of-control, meanest, surest devil of a voice you ever heard screamed 'Freeze, nigger, or I'll cut you in half!' I mean, anybody would have dropped in their tracks when they heard that, even if they hadn't been a... you know, black."

"They caught Bobby," Royce said. "Running from the scene with the gun in his hand."

She nodded forlornly. "They caught Bobby running from the scene. It turned out later he'd seen the police car coming and realized it was all over for him. So he just dropped the gun into the ditch and kept heading at the police car like he was jogging or something." She shook her head. "He did actually have a sweat suit on, and running shoes and a headband. He was skinny enough to be a jogger, too. Of course, there were a few miles of tracks up and down both arms at that time."

Royce feigned mild surprise. "Really? Last time I saw him I watched him pick up—"

Whoops. Watch it, Royce, he said to himself, you almost said he picked up two of the guards trying to strap him down so you could put a couple of intravenous needles in him. Royce looked at the bottle on the table next to him. He'd drunk a pint of Old Overholt and about a quarter of this fifth. He hadn't slept in a long time. Staying on his toes was getting difficult.

Yet here, now, he was getting the story he'd come to discover.

He sat up straight and curled his fists towards his chest. "Hell, they must have weighed close to three hundred pounds."

"What did," she asked distantly.

"Those barbells. The only exercise they'd let him take the whole time he was on Death Row was supervised solitary gymnasium type workouts, with weights, shooting basketball, stuff like that. He looked terrific the last time I saw him."

She looked puzzled. "You mean with muscles and all that stuff?"

Royce nodded.

"Yeesh," she said.

"Well," he said, "it's like mind control when you're inside. You have to do something, get focused on something, be disciplined."

"I guess so," she said.

"Cigarette?"

"Thanks."

He lit her Salem. Royce held the match before his pursed lips and blew on it gradually, increasing his wind until it went out. "Speaking of doing something," he said, dropping the match in an ashtray, "what happened to you and Eddie?"

Colleen stared into space.

"Do you mind my asking?"

"What?"

"It's a good story, you know."

"Yeah," she sighed, "I guess it is."

"So is it over?"

"Sorry. I'm kind of running out of gas. It was a long time ago.

The idea of Bobby Mink with muscles kind of confuses me."

"Thurman liked to say Bobby was 'humpy.'"

She smiled and smoked her cigarette.

Royce waited.

Then she said, "There was a dumpster."

"A dumpster?"

She smiled distantly. "Behind the store. I don't think Eddie ever had the slightest intention of running away. I do think he was surprised to see Bobby waiting for us out back. If Eddie had been the lookout, and it had been Bobby and me coming out that window, we never would have seen Eddie again. But there Bobby was. Like I said, Eddie is the kind of guy who can improvise as he goes along. Anything to leave behind a trail of confusion and himself in the clear. When he saw Bobby standing there, he got rid of the gun. Simple as that. He saw the dumpster on the way out the window, and another solution offered itself. Anything to avoid the same cliche Bobby was about to provide the story with, of running directly into the arms of the cops. Not Eddie. Eddie is into a high form of dance called survival. Since Bobby was into getting himself caught by hanging around and being useless, Eddie helped him out and at the same time turned him into something useful. Very useful. Bobby gave the cops everything they wanted. They didn't even take the trouble to look for anybody else. Bobby spent a year in jail before the trial, and then got convicted by a mess of people who assumed from the beginning he was in that robbery and killed that woman solo, all by himself, no help, alone."

She shook her head and blew smoke into the air between them. "It was all Eddie's fast thinking, and it handed Bobby the rawest deal you can imagine: first degree murder with special circumstances, the death penalty. But Bobby never ratted on Eddie because he thought I did it."

"What good would it have done if he had?" Royce asked. "They had nothing on either one of you. It would have been Bobby's word against you and Eddie."

She looked at him. "That old fan he tore out of that window was the greasiest thing you ever saw. It must have been blowing flies out the back of that building since Bob Wills was born. They could have lifted a clear set of prints of Eddie's right hand any time they wanted, at least until somebody got around to fixing that fan, and probably after. All they did, I'm sure, was nail it back up. I'll bet you a dollar that to this day there's Fast Eddie fingerprints in the grease around the sheet-metal shroud of that old exhaust fan."

"Well, why in hell didn't they find any fingerprints in the first place?"

She blew a smoke ring. "There were no witnesses, that's why. From the beginning the cops assumed Bobby had pulled the job by himself. When they matched the prints on the gun to him, and the ballistics matched the bullets in the clerk to the gun," she snapped her fingers, "bingo. They had their man."

Royce thought it was appropriate to say something. "Idiots," he said.

"Idiots? Idiots?" She stabbed the cigarette in his direction. "They didn't even run a paraffin test on him, to see if he'd fired the goddamn gun. Hell, the goddamn test was invented in Mexico, by a Mexican cop. If the Mexicans can invent the goddamn test, you'd think these cracker Dallas cops could use it. But no. Hell, no. They had their desperate Negro junkie and the murder weapon. Since he happened to have nine dollars on him at the time, they figured that's what he'd stolen, that's what he'd killed that woman for. The nine bucks made the crime that much more revolting." She sat up and crushed the cigarette in the ashtray. Royce's eyeballs itched with fatigue. He could see the night beginning to pale toward dawn in the bedroom window beyond Colleen. "But what am I complaining about?" She gestured broadly. "Between Bobby Mink's noble integrity and the racist incompetence of the cops, Eddie and I are still walking around. Ain't that a ethical dichotomy made in hell?"

"Ethical dichotomy?" Royce made a face. "Where'd you get a notion like that?"

"Hey, I'm cool," she said bitterly. "I been to night school."

Royce looked at her. Night school. "And Bobby?" he asked after a moment.

"Bobby?" She gave him a sharp look, then looked away. "Bobby's in a better place. Even if he's nowhere, he's in a better place."

"I knew he was innocent," Royce said bitterly. She nodded sadly. A tear bumped along her rough cheek.

He'd noticed that the more the effects of whatever drug she'd done earlier wore off, the sharper her mind became.

This is not to say that she'd become optimistic. Just sharper. Less vulgar. Or, should he say, less colloquial. And where's the surprise in that? In any case Royce yawned and thought it ironic she was waking up just as he was passing out. But, since a shot of heroin wears off after awhile, and alcohol has a progressively overwhelming effect if you persist in drinking it all night, there was no surprise, no irony, no twist of fate either. Just two ships passing in the night. Yeesh, as she'd said. He was just tired. Very tired. Now he could get vulgar and colloquial.

"But wait," he said through his yawn, blinking his eyes. "You mean to tell me you and Eddie jumped in a dumpster out back of that store and were never discovered?"

She lit another cigarette. "Never discovered. It was on the back side of the building, away from the street, and maybe fifty feet toward a dirt embankment from the window under a big cottonwood, and completely dark. Eddie threw me over the side and followed me in. It was perfect. The thing was full of empty cardboard boxes and beer cartons nobody had bothered to flatten like I guess they're supposed to. It was big, too, you could've hid five or six people in there. We just burrowed into the boxes toward the bottom and pulled several layers of them over the top of us. It was pitch-black and pretty funky in there, but not by the standards of a Dallas jailhouse."

"They must not have looked too hard for you."

She nodded and smoked. "They were out there all right, after they found the fan torn off the window. But the dirt was hard on account of about fifty years of bottle caps ground into it. Are you old enough to remember when sodas came in bottles, and the drink boxes had an opener on the side, and with a can underneath to catch all the bottle caps?"

Royce nodded.

She blew smoke and waved her hand at it. "I'm not. But the ground all around that old store was paved with bottle caps, like small cobblestones. Anyway, the point is there were no tracks to follow or anything. They looked around with flashlights and all. We lay there in the dark not talking, hardly moving, even after Eddie got his thing into me—"

Royce opened his eyes. "What?"

"Well, hell," she waved her cigarette, "we were there all night. For all we knew it was our last chance. I was pretty upset. He had to calm me down. Besides, Eddie bores easy."

"I thought you were Bobby's girl."

She looked at him.

After a moment he shook his head. "All night?"

"Pretty much. We could hear the radios squawking and cars come and go. There was an ambulance, lots of sirens. The worst moment was when some big vehicle pulled right up to the dumpster, after we'd been in there at least an hour. It didn't sound like it, but our worst scenario was of course the garbage truck had come to empty the trash. We could just see ourselves getting lifted up on those forks and inverted over the back of some huge rolling garbage compactor. Me with my pants down, Eddie with his thing hanging out...." She gave a short laugh. Royce had to smile.

"Then of course, we got compacted to death. Or arrested. Or shot. Or all three."

"What was it?"

"Television truck. Remote unit. The sound we heard was the antenna going up. We got out of there about noon the next day. By then it had gotten pretty bad. It was real hot, of course, and both of us had had to piss a couple of times by then, right where we lay. And we couldn't smoke, either. Yeah, I remember that; we couldn't smoke. Pretty funky. Got home and watched the whole thing on the evening news." She waved her hand toward the television set. "Just like tonight."

They looked at the television. A row of five men arranged

according to their varying heights and all dressed alike stood before the camera with their mouths open, obviously singing something. A telephone number appeared low on the screen in front of them, with the words GRACEPHONE above it and CALL NOW below it.

"Hey," she said, not taking her eyes off the screen, the cigarette in her hand close to her face, "I've had enough stress and pain for one night. Want to get high and go to bed?"

· THIRTEEN ·

For just a moment Royce couldn't believe his ears. But his ears weren't the problem. The problem was his desires. They conflicted. The last thing he wanted to do was a drug—any drug. Alcohol was fine with him; it was something he understood through long association. He knew what it would do to him, how and just about when. But the first thing he wanted to do, the thing uppermost on his agenda, was to sleep with Colleen Valdez.

To Colleen Valdez, the two went more or less together. You have drugs, that's O.K. You have sex, that's O.K. too. You have them together? You're on vacation. That was something Bobby Mencken used to say. He'd come home in the morning, after a hard night of crime, and he'd dangle a bag of dope in front of Colleen, and he'd say, "Let's take a vacation."

She might say "Sure," she might say "Break my arm," or she might pout and say "Make me," but the answer was always affirmative. Always.

That was the way it had been several years ago, when Colleen had been very much in love with Bobby Mencken. Everybody was younger; the whole world was younger. Exuberance was cheap and available in vast quantities, like gasoline in the fifties. But somewhere along the line things began to get more serious. The idea of money was everywhere, but the actual stuff became more and more of a rumor about something other people had somewhere else. Friends started to sicken and die from unnatural causes. Gunshot wounds, overdoses… lethal injections. She couldn't really put her finger on when suffering had replaced fun as the ongoing environment, just like she couldn't really put a finger on when junk became more important than anything else. Yet these things had transpired. It was as if one day she had looked up and noticed that somebody had moved all the scenery around in the theater since the last time she'd looked. The previous play, a comic farce, had closed. The new play, a tragic farce, had opened. As in the old play, the role she had in the new one was largely undefined. In the old play she'd been granted broad improvisational scope. In the new play, however, some force beyond her control, beyond her understanding, was always telling her what to do. And when to do it.

And now Eddie had bought the farm.

She was bored with all that snake business anyway.

It didn't even occur to her that Royce would be thinking twice about her offer. She stood up and said, "Come on. Let's take a vacation," and headed for the kitchen. Royce stayed where he was and watched her hips move in her jeans when she walked. "Don't worry," she said over her shoulder, "I know you don't go in for needlework." She chuckled.

"Yet."

Royce took his bottle and followed her.

The kitchen looked like the inside of a mobile home that'd rolled off a cliff and somehow landed upright. Books, pots, pans, bottles, magazines, newspapers and cans were everywhere. The cast-iron, formerly white sink was stained a dark rust color, its faucet hidden among stacks of glasses and dishes. There was a corrugated drainboard, chipped and stained, on either side of the sink, a small four-burner gas stove to its left, a very old refrigerator to the left of that, then a small table in the corner with two chairs. A door to the left of the table behind one of the chairs led to a small bathroom you had to step up into. To the left of that a dilapidated double-hung window looked out on the open-air entry hall, and appeared to have been painted last during the Depression, when people had time for such things. A dish towel with faded red and white checks had been tacked over it with two wood screws. The rest of the room was dirty yellow, and the whole thing looked like a video game for cockroaches.

On the table were several sections of various issues of the *Times-Herald* and the *Fort Worth Star-Telegram*, overflowing ashtrays, two half-empty Lone Star bottles with a cigarette butt in each, torn potato-chip bags and five dissimilar guitar picks arranged in a circle. In the center of these Royce placed the fifth of Ezra Brooks. One of the guitar picks fled, straight off the side of the table. Royce stamped at the roach and missed. Articles or parts of articles were circled in newspapers; some had pieces clipped out of them. Royce looked closely and saw that all were about Bobby Mencken's execution and the various appeals and legal maneuvering that had led up to it. As he peered at these, Royce noticed that his vision was blurred. He was drunker than he thought. He steadied himself by the table, then sat heavily on the chair beside the refrigerator.

"Take a load off your feet," Colleen said. A cigarette dangled from her mouth. She pursed the thick lips of her broad mouth around it, took a final drag and dropped the half-smoked cigarette into a glass in the sink, where it continued to smoke.

"Nice and domestic in here," Royce said tiredly, squinting up at the light bulb in the ceiling above him. He opened the refrigerator: a bottle of catsup missing its cap, a half bottle of Lone Star likewise, a can of tuna fish, a half jar of jalapeno peppers floating in discolored brine, two white take-out cartons with wire handles.

"I haven't eaten since I met you people," he said, closing the door.

She pulled a small packet from the watch pocket of her jeans and dropped it on the newspapers, along with a creased length of aluminum foil she'd taken from the back of the stove, and sat down in the other chair.

"You know how to do this, Royce?" she asked.

"Not so good as I know how to do the other," he said, attempting the lascivious.

"Yeah," she said absently, "I guess that makes you motivationally transparent."

"Come on," Royce said, drawing self-righteousness from a re-newed empathy with his role, "what kind of night school did you go to that taught you motivational transparence and no biology?"

"Hmph," she said, "all of them."

"Well," Royce pouted, "my testosterone has been on ice for over two years."

The packet had been torn from a picture magazine and cleverly folded into an envelope. She carefully opened it until it lay in a flat, colorful square on the table, about three inches on a side. An extremely thin line of beige powder lay along an inch and a half of the central crease.

"And I can eat better than I can do anything else," Royce said sullenly, eyeing the square of paper. "Is there anything there?"

"In a little while, you can tell me." With a knife she scraped about two-thirds of the powder onto the crease in the aluminum foil, thinning it out until the new line was about two inches long and evenly distributed. "Now watch me, Royce," she said.

"With pleasure," he said.

She held the aluminum foil folded in a slight V and made a couple of gentle passes beneath it with a butane lighter, closely watching the powder in the crease. The passes slowed. On the last one, a curl of thick smoke lifted from one end of the line of powder and followed the passage of the flame beneath the foil to the other end of the line, consuming the powder as it went. Her nose hovered about six inches above, and the smoke entered its flaring nostrils as she inhaled steadily, gently. Her nose followed the rising smoke across the sheet of aluminum foil until the smoke was gone. The lighter snapped off. Colleen inhaled deeply, held the breath, then sighed with satisfaction. Very little smoke came out with the exhalation.

Royce was fascinated. She had demonstrated great dexterity.

She took another deep breath and sighed.

"Now you," she said.

"Me?" he said.

She smiled sleepily at him. "Then both of us," she said dreamily.

Royce reached uncertainly for the aluminum foil.

"No," she said. "I'll do it all for you. You'd blow it."

"Oh," he said.

"No offense," she said, scraping the remainder of the powder onto the foil. "It's for your own good. Without the right touch it can go all at once and you lose the smoke. Or if it's too hot you can burn your lungs. It's too expensive to waste."

He watched her make an even line of the powder along the crease in the foil. Then he watched the lines of her breasts against the thin cotton cowgirl shirt as she leaned over the table. Once again her long black hair, tied back in the loosening braid, draped the side of her pockmarked face from her forehead across her cheek to her shoulder, and reminded him of a Pieta, a fond mother leaning over her blessed child. This idea of corrupt motherhood filled him with tenderness and lust, and it was as her willing student that he attentively positied his nose over the aluminum foil and inhaled deeply of the seductive fumes rising from it. The effect was almost immediate. He'd been drinking too much to be fooling around with heroin, not that it was dangerous in its present quantity, but the subtleties of its effects would be wasted on him. Or so he hoped. But a languid power diffused itself throughout his being and made a home there. He felt otherworldly, relaxed, sick and, curiously, as if he were party to a burgeoning integrity.

"How do you feel?" she asked.

He was gasping for air, a weightless yet hopeless victim of gravity. His eyes wouldn't stay open. "I feel bad," Royce said thickly.

"That's good," she said.

"I'd like to...to lie down..."

"Good idea," she whispered. "Let's."

His eyelids were sinking. He forced them open to look at Colleen. Her green eyes dwindled vertiginously to tiny dots as he watched them.

"It's not," Royce protested as she helped him up, "not what you think..." It was true, it wasn't what she thought. At least, it wasn't what he thought she thought. It wasn't that he didn't want to sleep with her; he did. Very much. It was just that, right now, he just wanted to lie down, just for a few minutes. Maybe right here on the floor. Go nose on nose with a roach. Then they could...He and Colleen... Later...

Then Royce realized that he was about to lose consciousness. Losing consciousness seemed like a good idea. He just wanted to lie down to do it.

Colleen got him to the bedroom and onto the bed. Daylight had happened already. He could feel the heat of the day beginning to rise from the city, but he was cool, more detached from the weather than he'd been in a long, long time.

He lay on the bed with his eyes closed while she moved about the room. He hadn't lost consciousness. Or had he? He felt no urgency to do anything. He just lay there with his eyes closed and soon the thought occurred to him that he was enjoying himself. He was very comfortable. Everything around him had gone to hell, or was going to hell, and that was fine; he was very comfortable, thank-you.

He began to think about things, languidly. He thought of Pamela screaming at him so loudly, so fiendishly that she became a soundless blur, vibrating on a frequency he couldn't clearly receive. He thought of Bobby Mencken's kiss, and in his mind he touched the lips Bobby's lips had touched. Royce didn't actually touch them. But in his mind he did. He saw the three people in the bar, glasses raised, looking at him, tacitly refusing to drink with a man who cynically raised his glass to the innocent and the guilty roasting alike in hell. He saw Johanson's red face, bloated in fury. He saw the faces of the witnesses watching him through the glass observation window of the gas chamber. They watched him without expression, their mouths slightly open, their faces pale against a pale green background. The reflections of the lights on the glass separating them from him wavered slightly, undulated gently along the horizontal. Then a small school of fish floated between Royce and the open-mouthed, pale faces of the death-chamber witnesses. The fish were almost transparent, with cobalt blue fins and bright yellow mouths and diagonal crimson streaks behind their eyes. They took their time swimming, a wiggle of a fin here, a flick of a tail there, and tilted to investigate the glass between themselves and the witnesses without fear. One turned to look at Royce. A bubble wavered upward from a gaping witness's mouth.

Only then did Royce realize they were all underwater. He laughed. It was a gentle laugh, because he had no energy for that sort of thing at all, but still it was a laugh. It felt good. Because, he realized, laughter is stronger than nausea. Everybody should feel this good, he thought, should feel more than nauseous. Then, of course, he wanted to cry, because he couldn't remember the last time he'd laughed. He realized it had been a long time, because he could feel the downward creases in his face resist the upward tendencies of his smile.

Far off, someone was handling him. He made slits of his eyes, or thought he did. Colleen pulled off one of his shoes for him. Then the other. Actually, he could see just fine, right through his eyelids in the dark.

"God, laces," she said. There was something about her, Royce thought, as he watched her leaning over him. He realized she was naked. Her skin was smooth and brown, like a coffee-colored beach with no footsteps. Her round breasts leaned with her, their nipples pointing at her work, like interested third parties. Her hair was loose and fell curling in spite of its length, past her shoulders and down her sides like a black cape.

She took off his socks. Then she came around the side of the bed opposite the window and unbuttoned Royce's shirt. He watched her closely. She was indeed a very beautiful woman. Royce had never seen such a beautiful unclothed body. And in spite of his narcosis he yearned for her. As she peeled his shirt off he fitted the palm of his hand to her buttocks and caressed the cleft between them.

"I have died," he said, as she backed away to slide the inverted sleeve of the shirt over his hand. He let the arm fall and smiled. "I have died and gone to malpractice heaven."

Then she unbuckled his belt and unzipped the zipper on his pants.

"Mmmm," she said dreamily, and kissed him. Royce was back in his seventeen-year-old mode.

"Pinch me," he said, weakly stroking her hair, "I must be dreaming." And she did, intimately.

She peeled the pants down over his legs and feet, one at a time, and dropped them to the floor at the end of the bed. Then she left the room.

"Where… ?" Royce protested, but he was too stoned to do

anything else. He'd been robbed of everything, apparently, but his virility. It was like an image without a context.

She reappeared bearing the whiskey bottle and set it on the floor next to his side of the bed.

"My side of the bed," Royce said quietly, watching her. "I like that."

Colleen said nothing. She lifted a leg over him and stepped onto the bed, then knelt and leaned toward the window. She had to stretch to reach the frayed hem of the curtain. The curtain looked like burlap, but Royce wasn't looking at the curtain. His hand probed her behind as she drew the rough cloth along the rod to cover the window. The room was cast into a shadowy obscurity.

Then Colleen turned around and showed things to Royce he'd only heard about in the prison hospital, from the convicts who had done them to each other.

· FOURTEEN ·

Three days after the bungled robbery, Colleen and Royce were still in bed.

Late the first day they'd left the apartment only long enough to buy more whiskey and heroin with Royce's money. He wouldn't let Colleen take it out in trade and insisted she pay cash for it. But it wouldn't be long before he'd have to let her do so, because he didn't have all that much cash.

So the second day he'd magically produced out of his Gladstone bag the bottle of pharmaceutical morphine and introduced her to it. She had never taken morphine before, and Royce was proud to be able to show this woman, who had been showing him so much, something new. She in turn introduced him to the practice of injecting the drug directly into a vein in his arm. He in turn converted her to the sanitary practice of disinfecting the site with isopropyl alcohol both before and after the injection, and the novel idea of using a fresh disposable diabetic syringe each time, of which he had a plentiful supply.

Colleen Valdez was very grateful for the morphine. She even began to allow Royce to inject her. After all, being a doctor, he was very good at it. Moreover, he immediately noticed a certain perverse thrill associated with the act of injecting her, which he could only liken to sexual foreplay. As for the rest of the formalities, the alcohol and the clean syringes and so forth, she merely put up with it to indulge him.

After all, he was the doctor. Colleen could play the patient. Or nursy, with Royce as the patient. There was plenty of time to work out the kinks.

Thus, for the next twenty-four hours they didn't leave the apartment at all. Later, she went out for an hour to buy whiskey and potato chips while Royce grabbed a little shut-eye.

By dusk on the third day Royce had been all over the place, so far as the bed was concerned, and was lying on his back again. Colleen knelt on top of him, her arms hooked under his shoulders, and they were slowly, very slowly, passing the time. Then Eddie Lamark came home.

He just appeared in the doorway to the bedroom. Royce wasn't really sure if he'd noticed Eddie before Eddie spoke.

He saw Eddie no longer had on the flowered shirt but a blue and white checked cowboy number, open to the waist. Sweat streaked his temples and cheeks, and he looked a little worse for wear, gaunt and tired. An unlit cigarette dangled from his mouth, and he stood in the doorway squinting through the gray twilight of the bedroom at the couple on the bed.

"Well, now," he drawled, "that's just about the prettiest thing I've seen all week."

As though dancing together without speaking, Royce and Colleen, lost in their private reflections, were both slow to react to the interruption. Royce enlarged the slits of his eyes enough to see the checked shirt through the hair falling over his face from the girl's shoulders and said nothing. Dimly he thought that, if Eddie still had his gun, Franklin Royce might be about to be history. A messenger bearing the scrolls of panic was dispatched from one part of his system to some other part, but was lost along the way, only to arrive shortly in the neighborhood of Royce's groin, where the information was scrambled into an unprecedented eroticism. Fear became drowned in renewed pleasure. To die now was to die in the saddle, in the throes of happiness, and he smiled and arched his back at the possibility.

Colleen noticed the redoubling of Royce's effort and reacted with a purring sound in her throat. She didn't even turn around when she said gently, with a distant note of surprise, "Eddie, you're back."

"No, your back," Eddie repeated, "is the prettiest sight I seen in three days." He was fiddling with his belt. "Don't get, up, Colleen honey," he added hastily. "Don't move; don't change a thing; I'll be right there."

Eddie left his pants where they fell and, unsnapping the bottom two buttons on the checked shirt, knelt on the bed behind Colleen. He wrapped two thick tresses of Colleen's long black hair around his fists like a stagecoach driver taking the reins for the long haul to El Paso.

"Giddap," he said. The unlit Salem was still clenched between his teeth.

Then the three of them began to do things Royce had only heard about in the prison hospital, from the convicts who did them to each other.

"The old woman met me on the first floor landing with a Colt .44," Eddie said later, as the three of them lay in bed smoking cigarettes, "a real antique." In the past couple of days Royce had taken to having a puff or two as Colleen smoked. "I'd been in the house less than a minute."

Eddie took a pull on Royce's bottle. "She never even asked me my name," he said. "The lights suddenly came on and there she was, about ten steps up the staircase. She just started blowing holes in the wall behind my head."

"The tube said she only fired once," Royce said.

Eddie passed the bottle to Royce. "You got to get hip to the notion that there's a ten percent margin of error, *minimum,*" Eddie shook a finger at the ceiling, "in all television, newspaper, and radio reportage. That's minimum, and don't get me started."

"Sure," said Royce, "O.K.," thinking, goddamn know-it-all.

"She got off at least two," Eddie continued, "and she probably wasn't a bad shot, either. She was scared, so her aim was shaky. Hell, I was scared too." He drew on his cigarette and exhaled smoke into the air before them. Outside the open window beyond Eddie, a faraway dog yapped and a car horn distantly sounded one long, two short.

"But the scareder I get, the straighter I shoot," Eddie said.

"Plus you got experience," Royce added. Colleen pinched him.

Eddie turned toward Royce in the gloom, looked at him for a moment, looked at Colleen, then looked away. Another moment passed. "Yeah," Eddie said finally.

Aha, Royce thought to himself. Colleen and I have a secret, and she wants to keep it that way. Come to think of it, so does Eddie. Her hand rested over his thigh where she'd pinched him. He nonchalantly covered it with his hand and gave it a reassuring squeeze. She drew hers away and pointed behind him.

"Reach me that ashtray, Royce," she said.

He looked at her a moment, then retrieved a peanut can heaped with butts and pull-tabs from the inverted wooden keg that served as a nightstand next to the bed. It was the kind of little barrel, bound in iron hoops, that horseshoes used to come in. Royce studied the keg and held the can while Colleen rubbed out the glowing end of her cigarette. Pamela's uptown blacksmith made house calls out of a brand new Winnebago fitted out as a smithy. He towed a modest forge complete with electric bellows on a small trailer behind it. There was an anvil on the back bumper. He dealt horseshoes to his customers a few at a time out of a selection of such kegs, and the bills were extravagant, at least twice what a working ranch might expect to be charged. Moreover, the man liked to make broad insinuations about the favors of certain lonely equestriennes. The blacksmith was a big, hairy bastard, his arms littered with scabbed burns from working the forge, and Royce hated him.

He thoughtfully replaced the ashtray. Why should he ever have to lay eyes on that sonofabitch again?

He'd been gone from home for four or five days. It was highly unlikely that anyone would ever think of looking for him in this part of Dallas. Pam could have the house—a court would give it to her anyway; hell, her Daddy had put the down payment on it. She could have the ranch, the animals, the blacksmith, the whole stinking life. Most of all, she could have herself.

He settled back against the pillow behind him. His bare leg lay against Colleen's. He regarded the taper of her body for a moment and thought, I like it here.

Eddie belched loudly. Royce's eyes skipped over Colleen's smooth thighs to Eddie's pale hairy ones beyond. He had knobby knees.

"As Marlon Brando said, 'She didn't give me no selection, Dad.'"

Eddie sniffled and rubbed the flat of his hand up across his nostrils. "After the gunplay there was at least twenty minutes before you all were supposed to come back, and she and I must have sounded like Beirut at midnight, banging away at each other in there. There was nothing to do but flee. I took a chance and looked in the garage. The keys were in the switch and an electric garage door opener was clipped to the sunshade. Nice car, too, a new Buick. It was so well laid out I thought it was a trap." He snapped a fist at the air in front of him, as if catching a fly. "It wasn't, though."

Nobody said anything. Royce fingered the two festering disks Eddie had burned into his neck. Each was about a quarter-inch across with a thick crust on it.

"But what about the shirt, Eddie," Colleen asked curiously. "Said on the tube the police arrested a man wearing a flowered shirt like somebody saw driving that Buick away from the Greyson house."

Royce leaned forward and grinned knowingly. "That part of that ten percent margin of error?"

Eddie nodded sagely. "Depends on how you look at it, Royce," he said, clasping both his hands behind his head and leaning back against the wall, with the filter of a Salem clenched between his teeth. "I tore out of there backwards, all the way down to the street. Then I headed back the way you all were supposed to come from, thinking that with some luck I'd intercept you on the way back, or waiting on a corner some place. Then I could have switched cars almost immediately and they'd never have found us."

"Smart," Royce said uneasily. But he was thinking, what does he mean they'd never have found us. *Have* they found us?

Colleen lit another cigarette and blew a smoke ring between them.

Eddie shook his head. "Just a dumb idea I had, like watching your number on the wheel of fortune. Trouble with hopes like that is, you're still staring at your number after the wheel has stopped and they've taken your money away. Then they take *you* away. Can I get a witness?"

"Hallelujah," Royce said uncertainly.

"Tell it," Colleen said.

"You got to play the combinations." Eddie spoke with conviction.

"That's if you're taking chances," Royce said.

"Right on," Eddie said dryly. "We're only talking about people who take chances in the first place."

Colleen laughed.

"So by then I'm cutting along Walnut Hill, and a police car comes hauling the other way with all its lights going. I realize I'm going way too fast and slow it down a bit. There's this Seven-Eleven out there."

Colleen nodded.

"I pull through and take a look around. There's a kid coming out of the store with a six-pack and he heads over to the corner of the parking lot. There's an old-model red MG parked there with the top down, clean as a whistle. By the time he's got the bag in the passenger seat, I'm over there asking him for directions to Balch Springs, which you dig is to hell and gone clear across town.

"He starts to point and shakes his head. Them directions is not going to be easy. So he comes over between the cars to give me the details. I'm wiping my prints off the steering wheel with my shirttail. He even squats down. I touch the tip of his nose with the muzzle of the .25. He can smell all nine bullets I just fired out of it. 'Get in,' I say, and slip the door latch and slide a little ways over the seat."

Royce frowned. "Nine?"

"A couple of them missed her," Eddie said defensively.

"So it was empty?"

"Emptier'n the average middle-class life," Eddie said. "But the kid don't know that, of course. Anyhow, the smell of powder makes him weak. I know it does that to me."

"Gives me a headache," Colleen volunteered.

Eddie shifted his eyes to her, snorted derisively, then went on with his story, staring straight ahead as if there were a hologram of the events in the gloom beyond the foot of the bed.

"The kid is about nineteen and scared shitless; he gets in. 'Close the door.' He closes the door. I get his money and his car keys. 'Nice shirt.' He's doesn't know what's up. 'Trade shirts.' He looks at me like I'm crazy. 'Yes,' I nod at him over the gun, 'I'm crazy, but I don't want to hurt you. The shirt.' We trade shirts.

"It takes just a minute. Another police car goes by toward University Park, all its lights and the siren on. 'Nice shirt, nice car.' I held up his wad of bills. 'How much is here?' 'I don't know,' he says, 'maybe two hundred.' 'What's a kid like you doing with two hundred dollars in his pocket, huh?' He's staring straight over the wheel and shrugs. 'Huh?' 'I don't kn-know!' he yells, stuttering like.

"'O.K.,' I say, 'You don't know, you can afford to lose it. Here's the deal. You restore that MG yourself?' 'Yes.' Perfect. 'Want to see it again?' He looks at me. 'Look, mister, you got a nice Buick here, how come—' 'Shut up.' 'Please—' 'Don't beg, boy, it ain't manly. I got a deal here for you. I keep the red car and the two hundred.' He grits his teeth. 'You, I say, 'keep your life.'"

Eddie chuckled. "We're talking in the car like a couple of guys waiting for our girlfriends to quit looking at magazines in the Seven-Eleven. 'But you got to do me a favor.' 'What kind of favor.' 'Nothing much,' I say, 'a little driving.' 'Driving?' 'Driving…'"

Royce stifled a yawn. It had been a couple of hours since he and Colleen had taken a shot, and the morphine was wearing off. He scratched himself listlessly. Since yesterday, every time he came down he'd noticed a small hunger, a quiet, persistent yearning, and until he had another shot he was irritable. He recognized it as a hunger for the drug, but so long as they had the drug he was willing to indulge it. It was true that the hunger for the drug was worse than the hunger for food. He was a little disconcerted by this. Moreover, the craving for food could always be traced to the stomach and thus easily defined. The source of hunger for the drug was less traceable, it seemed to come from some place much deeper, more profound than the stomach, and at the same time the hunger seemed to be more generally dispersed throughout his entire system. He smiled. Maybe it came from his soul. More likely, and more terribly, it came from his metabolism. No hedonist can find the strength to deny his own metabolism; his soul, yes, but not his metabolism.

He noticed Colleen idly passing the flat of her hand back and forth along her forearm. She was probably much more strung out than Royce was. From injecting her he'd discovered many scarred veins in both her arms. One particularly bad one felt like a length of twig embedded beneath her skin. An equal dose of morphine had a much milder effect on her than it did on himself. She generally required a quarter to a third increase over his dose.

Now there was a new problem. As soon as Eddie stopped blabbing and paid attention to what was going on around him, he would be cutting into their supply. Courtesy would demand it, wouldn't it? Would Colleen resent that as much as Royce would? Could she be as disgusted by Eddie as Royce was, too? Did these people react to anything? He reached out and took her cigarette from her. She watched him take a puff, and for a moment their eyes met. The contact was soundless, but Royce could feel her green gaze penetrate to the very roots of his sexuality. A third kind of hunger. He'd never felt like this about a woman before. Lustful. Possessive. Protective. Jealous, maybe? He proffered her cigarette. Her fingers briefly entwined with his. His sex stirred. He exhaled smoke thoughtfully at it. She took the cigarette.

"Eddie," she said. "What happened to the kid?"

Eddie stopped talking.

Royce sat very still. The room became very silent. Through the open window the neighborhood had momentarily fallen silent; they could hear a jet taking off from Love Field, six or eight miles away.

· FIFTEEN ·

Eddie laughed. "What the hell you mean, baby? Give me a cigarette."

"Royce has them."

Royce found the package of Salems on the keg and offered it. Eddie took one. He put the filter to his lips and lit the end with the butt of the previous one, inhaled deeply, exhaled. He moved the window curtain aside with his foot and flicked the butt out the open window. The curtain fell back into place. "Nice to be home fucking and fighting again, baby. It was touch and go there for a couple days." He inhaled and exhaled smoke again.

"Man, Eddie," Colleen said, "I don't know how you do it."

Eddie smoked some more. Then he asked, "What's got you two so straight anyway?"

Don't tell the mother, Royce thought.

Colleen ran her hand up and down the inside of Royce's thigh. "Royce here happens to have a stash, Eddie," she said brightly. "We saved some for you, too." She looked at Royce. Royce looked at her. *Damn.* But the green eyes and their black lashes in the pitted face, framed by the oval of obsidian hair, might have run an empire, on another planet. A planet of Royces. "Didn't you, Royce?" She patted his knee encouragingly.

"Yeah," he said sullenly.

"Royce knows how to make himself welcome."

"That I do, Eddie," Royce said, uncertain as to what occasion he was rising. He cleared his throat. "Ever tasted morphine?"

"No, really?" Eddie said, his eyes lighting up like a child's. "You have M? Genuine M?"

"The best, right out of the hospital," Colleen said proudly. "This guy Royce is a gift, Eddie. A gift, straight from Bobby Mink."

Eddie turned and looked at her, then at Royce. For a moment he chewed his lip uncertainly, "Good old Bobby Mink," he said softly.

Royce's eyes hardened. "Yeah," he said, "good old Bobby Mink." The nerve of this guy Lamark, he thought. There's not a principle in him.

"It's a little old," Colleen said apologetically, patting Royce's knee some more. "It was in Royce's doctor bag the whole time he was in stir. His wife never even thought to look in there."

Eddie smiled uncomfortably. "Probably out selling her ass for it the whole time," he said vaguely.

"How ironic," Colleen agreed.

Royce stood up out of the bed. An odor of sweat and stale tobacco rose with him. He self-consciously stood up straight, so his gut wouldn't look so fat to Colleen. Or to Eddie. "Hard to believe some people can do without the stuff," he said primly, and turned to the other two, still lying together on the bed. "Three hits of M, with legs?" he said cheerfully.

"Well, I'll be damned," Eddie said. "I never would've of thought you had it in you."

"Wait till you get an armful of this stuff, Eddie," Colleen said. "It's more fun than a new pony."

Royce smiled good-naturedly. "In you's where it's going, Eddie," he said. "I'm just grateful you didn't snake-bite me when you found me in bed with your best girl."

Eddie shrugged. "What's wrong with that?" he said. "I get my kicks."

"Kootchie-kootchie," Colleen giggled.

"Really?" Royce asked, disgusted.

Eddie held his cigarette hand up, palm outward toward Royce. "Ten or twelve milligrams ought to just about handle it," he said.

"Is that all?" Royce said as he turned and left the room.

"Yowsah," Eddie said happily. "The groceries are on me."

"I'll take you up on that," Royce said from the other room.

"Eddie," he heard Colleen say, "tell me truly, you lying bastard. How'd you manage it?"

"Aw," Eddie said, "I just let somebody steal the car, that's all. Easiest thing in the world."

"You let somebody steal the car?" she said incredulously. "How in the world … ?"

"Then I checked into a motel for a couple of days, just till I could be sure the coast was clear." He paused.

Watching us the whole time, Royce thought as he stood in the living room, to see if the cops were onto us.

"I knew you didn't let some kid get a load of you with your shirt off," she said. "These tattoos would have killed one or the other of you."

"Sure," Eddie said. "Hey, does this tickle?"

She giggled. "So where'd you get the money for a motel?"

"Ah, forget it," he said gruffly. "That whiskey still around?"

Royce listened to this conversation as he pulled the Gladstone bag from behind the couch. She's real chatty with him, he thought sourly, more than she is with me. The dim living room was illuminated only by the light of the television, its sound turned all the way down. His eyes fell on the short-brimmed sweat-stained beige Stetson he'd left there days ago. It was as if he'd never seen it before. He swept it along with several empty potato-chip bags onto the floor and set the bag on the table. He sat on the couch and busied himself with the paraphernalia.

He could hear the edginess in Eddie's voice, but he couldn't be sure if Eddie was nervous about the possibility of a fix after going four days without, or about the vagueness of his own story. But Royce soon tuned out the voices in the bedroom, only half listening to their chatter. He had other things on his mind. He'd decided it was time for Eddie to go.

Colleen had spilled the story. Even though Bobby had been mixed up with the store robbery, had in fact been up to his neck in it, Eddie had allowed him to go down for the murder Eddie himself had committed. Eddie had in fact set Bobby up for the fall. He'd set up his best friend, and incidentally Colleen's lover, by counting on the fact that Bobby would try to help them out of a jam. Well, he'd helped them all right. And in the process he'd helped himself all the way to Death Row.

Moreover, it wouldn't be long before Eddie took a second look at Royce.

He took a box of diabetic syringes out of his bag and noisily tore three of them out of their paper packages. These were narrow syringes with very short, small needles on them, twenty-six gauge. Intended for use by diabetics, to inject insulin with a minimum of discomfort, they were ideal for injecting certain other products, too. Morphine, for example. Royce placed the serum bottle of morphine on the table in front of him. Also suitable, he thought, for injecting an overdose of morphine, or—he removed another bottle from the Gladstone bag and placed it on the table beside the first—for injecting a judicious cocktail of Pavulon, potassium chloride and sodium thiopental.

No sense wasting all that morphine.

He took a bottle of alcohol, a couple of balls of cotton and a length of surgical tubing out of the bag.

Then he sat there for a moment and fingered the bullet hole in the Gladstone bag. The bullet hole of integrity. The Hippocratic ricochet. Many thoughts passed through his mind. Among them, that Royce had never killed anyone, even by mistake.

Eddie Lamark, on the other hand, had been directly responsible for killing at least two people that Royce knew of, both of them women, both of them more or less defenseless. Royce found it hard to believe that a seventy-year-old grandmother could be any match for a man as ruthless as Eddie Lamark, even with a Colt .44. Moreover, Eddie had been indirectly responsible for Bobby Mencken's death. Indirectly, Royce thought, by the slimmest margin of the definition of the word. Eddie had tricked and betrayed Bobby into the death chamber, knowing that Bobby would never return the favor, even if he could.

That made three people Eddie had killed.

Royce was in a position to return the favor in kind.

Moreover, Royce wanted Colleen Valdez—all of her, all to himself. The very thought of watching her again in Eddie's embrace…

Not to mention the threat Eddie no doubt would sooner than later pose to Royce's own welfare....

He fingered the two small burns on his neck. On the television in front of him the starship Enterprise slid out of orbit. The Revenge of the Branded...

It was time for Eddie to go.

Taking up one of the hypodermics, Royce removed the protective plastic sleeve from the needle, penetrated the rubber cap of the death serum, and depressed the plunger. He inverted the bottle over the syringe and watched it slowly fill by the light of the television beyond. He removed the needle with its telltale squeak.

From the bedroom came the sound of liquid sliding from one end of a bottle to the other and back. "Hey," Eddie said, "you getting off by yourself in there?"

"Sorry," Royce said, silently placing the serum bottle on the table top and taking up the bottle of morphine. "Star Trek's on."

He heard Colleen's titter.

"Too much, man," Eddie said.

"Right there," Royce said, drawing morphine into the second syringe. How was he going to tell the hypodermics apart? Both solutions showed clear in the syringes.

"Who's first?" Royce said. He placed the morphine-filled syringe on the left side of the table and removed the cap from the third, empty one. There was a knot in his stomach. Can't do it with the fluid levels; that's too obvious.

"I'm O.K.," Colleen said lazily. "Let Eddie get off first. He's been out working. I wanna see his face when it hits him."

"Solid," Eddie said doubtfully.

"Let Royce hit you, Eddie," Colleen said. Royce held the bottle inverted before the television and watched the fluid level in the syringe. His hands were damp and shaking.

"What am I, helpless?" Eddie barked.

"That's O.K.," Royce lied. "He doesn't have to do that."

"No, you're really good at it," Colleen said loudly. Then she was saying, "Let him," in a softer voice. "He really is a doctor."

Royce could almost see Eddie curl his lip and shrug a shoulder. "Sure," he said, "let's see if he can hit me clean the first time."

"Hey," Colleen said in the louder voice, "a challenge. Guy in here with his veins petrified like plastic water pipes."

"I'll bring the hollow drill." The needle, Royce thought, taking up the deadliest syringe, bend the needle. Take them all in there, in case he's wise. He laid the tip of the needle almost flat against the red rubber cap of the morphine bottle and pressed. Sweat rolled into his left eye and stung it. He knew the needle was decently strong, but it was also brittle and might easily snap. He relaxed the pressure and looked. The needle was straight. He applied it again to the cap and pressed harder. He felt it yield. He snatched it away from the bottle and rotated the syringe in the light of the television. The needle had a slight crook to it, right where it joined the sleeve affixed to the syringe.

"They're landing on Altair," Royce said, without looking at the television. He placed the syringe alongside the other two. "Just as we're leaving." Though he knew the poisoned syringe was on the right, he couldn't tell them apart. He rolled the three of them back and forth. The needle on the poisoned one wobbled and stood out clearly.

Just in case, he thought to himself, and he snatched up the three syringes in his left hand, the hot one uppermost.

In his other hand he gathered the brown bottle of alcohol and cotton swabs, the amber length of rubber tubing. He took a deep breath and entered the bedroom door.

Colleen and Eddie were kissing. Each of them held a lit cigarette with the other's shoulder in one hand, and the other's hip in the other hand.

Royce's jaw tightened. This was going to be easier than he'd thought. He might even take some pleasure in it. But maybe not. Justice can be a sobering thing. "Nice bilateral symmetry," he said grimly, crossing to Eddie's side of the bed. "You want to get off this way or that way?"

Eddie immediately broke the clinch with Colleen. "Oh," he said, "so many choices." He took a last drag on his cigarette and handed it to her.

"Just make yourself comfortable, Eddie," Colleen said. "Pretend Royce is a pharmaceutical geisha." Royce bowed from the waist. He laid the three syringes on the windowsill and screwed the cap off the bottle of alcohol.

Colleen caught Royce's eye. "This morphine kick is great, Eddie," she said enthusiastically. "No cooking or running out of matches, no blackened spoons, no looking for little bits of cotton, no clogged points—not even dull ones. And best of all," she snapped her fingers, "no copping: home delivery."

"Yeah," Eddie said. He was massaging the inside of his right elbow and working the arm up and down, paying her little attention.

"Here," Royce said, "I'll handle that."

Eddie looked at him strangely. Then he looked at Colleen. "Don't I get a sucker, Doc?" Eddie looked at Royce again.

Colleen smacked her lips. "Later Eddie," she said impatiently. "Let's get off."

Royce wrapped Eddie's thin bicep with the surgical tubing. "Make a fist."

"Make a fist," Eddie mocked him. But he sat back against the wall at the head of the bed with his arm alongside his thigh and made a fist. The outsized black widow tattooed along Eddie's forearm undulated over his musculature. Royce felt the inside of the elbow. The veins would be calloused from years of abuse, but Royce had taken blood samples from dozens of convicts with similar problems. He skillfully found a pulsing vein and rolled it beneath his thumb. He passed the alcohol swab over the area. Eddie's flesh was a pale ochre beneath the tattoos; it reacted slowly to Royce's touch, like soft wax.

Royce looked up. Eddie's eyes were fixed on the injection site with a fascinated stare. There was a slight yellowish tinge to their whites.

Hepatitis, Royce thought. Remind me to wash my hands.

"Ready, Eddie?"

Eddie looked Royce in the eye and sneered. "What do you mean, 'ready'?"

Exactly what Bobby Mencken had said. This almost unnerved Royce, but he kept his gaze steady. He could feel Eddie's pulse beneath the tip of his thumb. In his right hand, held the way a Frenchman holds his cigarette, Royce held the thin hypodermic that would turn Eddie to dust.

There is always the question, Royce thought, of how little or how much a man shooting dope hates himself.

"I know you're ready, Eddie," he said gently. "It's just habit, I guess. Like the lollipop and the smile." There was indeed an odd ghost of guileless habit in this deadly tableau, as Royce smiled his most natural bedside smile.

Eddie's sneer curled into a snarl. "Fuck your lollipop and your smile," he said.

Royce stiffened. His smile faded.

Colleen whined. "Eddie…"

Royce looked down at Eddie's arm. The gleaming tip of the needle lay against the unpunctured skin. The veins were beginning to swell from the tourniquet above. How to handle this? Royce straightened up.

"Maybe you don't like morphine," he said. His smile had become a thin line on his face. "Maybe I should just throw the hit out the window here. What would be the difference?"

Eddie stared rigidly at Royce. A wet line of perspiration glistened at his temple.

"He's just like that, Royce," Colleen said in a plaintive voice. "He likes to upset people; it's automatic with him. He sees you smile, it makes him unhappy. When you're unhappy, he's smiling. Quite a gig, huh? Not much, a little obvious, but it's his. And he's uptight about something. Come on, Eddie," she said tenderly, smoothing his hair, touching his arm, "get off and relax. You don't have to tell us where you've been…."

Eddie stared at Royce. Then he blinked. "Yeah," he said suddenly. He exhaled, two short puffs. "Yeah." He sighed and relaxed slightly against the wall. "Yeah…"

Colleen looked at Royce and nodded toward the syringe. "Must have been rough," she said soothingly, touching Eddie's brow at the hairline. "Shooting that woman in the—" She stopped abruptly. "You know."

Eddie glanced at her. "Yeah," he said, looking away. "I know all about it." He worried the corner of his mouth with the tip of his tongue and watched Royce cleanly hit the side of the vein and lever the length of the needle in, an arrow toward the heart. Nice work. Eddie's blood flowered into the syringe and Royce loosened the surgical tubing. "So you're a friend of Bobby Mink's," Eddie said. "He ever mention me?"

Royce nodded as the plunger bottomed into the syringe. "Yeah," he said, withdrawing the needle from the puncture. "A good friend." He placed the cotton swab over the drop of blood that appeared there and looked up. Eddie's jaw had begun to sag and his lips were going slack. A tiny frown was beginning to invent itself in the creases around his eyes. "He told me that if I ever did run into to you, I was to give you this," Royce said.

He leaned forward and kissed Eddie on the mouth.

"Bobby. . . ?" Eddie whispered. "I didn't…" His face began to slowly oscillate between the frown and a blank. Colleen sat back on her heels and continued to stroke his brow. Eddie tried to breath deeply once and almost got it in. But he was suffering from pulmonary arrest; his mechanism for processing air was collapsing. The second breath was abrupt and incomplete. Eddie opened his mouth and tried to yawn but couldn't. He relaxed against the wall at the head of the bed, much as he had been for the past hour, and died with his eyes open.

• SIXTEEN •

"Oh, Eddie," Colleen said, looking sadly at the dead man, stroking his short hair. "Eddie, Eddie, Eddie."

Royce put the spent syringe on the windowsill with the two others. His hands were shaking, and sweat ran down his naked ribs from both armpits. He pushed the dead man's legs out of the way and sat heavily on the edge of the bed. A spring cracked musically beneath the mattress. The damp, wrinkled sheets had a gritty feeling to them. No air moved through the open window. From beyond the back steps and clotheslines of the buildings this window looked out on, he heard the emphatic beat of a radio in a passing car. Somewhere somebody was stacking dishes and flatware. He looked at Eddie. Eddie stared sightlessly at him.

"Eddie, Eddie, Eddie," he said softly. He looked at Colleen Valdez. "How did you know?"

She ignored the question. She reached out and tentatively touched Eddie's hair, then withdrew the hand.

Royce dully watched her breasts. Now what, he wondered. He felt annoyed. And now, what not? After all, he'd just killed a man. That's what he'd come here to do, wasn't it? Well, no, not really. He'd come here to find out who framed Bobby Mencken. And he found out. Eddie had framed Bobby Mencken. He looked at Colleen. "How did you know, Colleen?" he said again. "You knew I was going to kill Eddie."

She continued to look at Eddie and make gentle, meaningless motions with her hands, reaching out to touch him, withdrawing the hand, reaching out again and tentatively touching him.

"You're stroking a corpse," Royce said cruelly.

She shot him a fierce glance. "And who the fuck are you?" she hissed.

He looked at her. She looked at him. Her look wavered. "Am I next?" she said.

"What?" he asked, incredulous. "You? No, never, no way."

She sat primly, for a naked woman, looking straight ahead at Eddie, and said, "That may be so. Anyway, I knew him for a long time. We were friends."

"He wasn't Bobby's friend," Royce argued. "I saw Bobby die and—" He stopped himself. Yes, Dr. Royce?

She continued to look at Eddie.

"And Eddie framed him," Royce blundered onward. "You told me so yourself."

"Eddie took care of me," she said quietly.

"So can I. Better care."

"He could play the guitar," she said tearfully.

"He was a scumbag," Royce growled. "Jesus Christ. You loved Bobby Mencken, remember? The man kissed me when he died!" Royce no longer cared about the continuity of his story. To hell with continuity. "I didn't hardly even know the guy and I could see he was innocent! Anybody could see it! I had to do something about it. So there he is." Royce shook a finger at Eddie. "There's the guy who killed Bobby Mencken. You loved Bobby. I could have loved Bobby. I mean, he was my friend. The guy who as good as murdered him is dead. It's called revenge! *Ain't it jut ducky?*"

Royce was shouting. He suddenly became aware that this was no ordinary domestic argument, such as he might have had with Pamela. He was naked, shouting over the naked corpse of a man he'd just murdered, at a naked female junkie, in a squalid Dallas tenement with lots of syringes and morphine and neighbors lying around. He looked at the open window and wondered if anyone could hear or understand him. He cursed under his breath and ground his teeth. They were going to have to do something with the body. He stood and looked out the window. Three stories below, in the darkness among several garbage cans, he could see the remains of the television set Eddie had thrown over the stairwell banister three days before. Around the narrow courtyard stood several buildings, some of them taller than the one he was standing in, with maybe fifty or sixty windows looking out on it. No good. They weren't going to be able to just throw Eddie out the window and go on living the simple life. It was going to take some work. He looked up. The lights of a few stars had managed to penetrate the glare of the huge city below them. Even so, it looked mighty clean up there. Did the stars know how dirty it was down here? Is that why they're so far away?

He pulled his head back in the window and thought about it. They were going to have to take that filthy living room rug out to get cleaned with Eddie rolled up in it. He looked beyond the bed at the rug in the living room, below the blue light of the television. Even from where he stood it was obvious that it was going to be hard to convince anybody that rug was worth doing anything to other than throwing it out. So O.K., that was it. They were going to take the rug to the dump and come home with a new one.

Of course, in this neighborhood, someone would come up to them and say, what you throwing away a perfectly good rug for? Eight Ball, maybe it would be Eight Ball. Give it here, he'd say. I'll take it home right now, be good for the baby to play on.

So there Royce and Colleen would be in the street, sweating under the dead weight of Eddie and the rug, trying to keep moving toward the pickup, trying to explain to Eight Ball or whoever that the rug had been quarantined and condemned and had to get incinerated by the government, no ifs, ands or buts; they were waiting at the dump for it now.

Maybe if they waited a couple of days for Friday night. Everybody would be too busy getting liquored up to worry about an old rug. But this was a hell of a climate to be leaving corpses lying around in.

He came wearily around to the other side of the bed. "Look, Colleen," he said patiently, quietly this time. She ignored him. He saw the whiskey bottle on the floor by the wooden keg. An amber buoy in a gray sea. That was what he needed. He picked it up and had a drink and lay down on the bed next to her.

Still she watched Eddie. Royce looked beyond her, at Eddie. His eyes were still open and so was his mouth, a fleck of foam at the corner of it. His tongue hadn't yet begun to push up behind his teeth, but it would soon enough. The tattoos blotched his arms, his head and neck, his shoulders. He was very pale beneath the blue checked shirt.

"Now we can call him Past Eddie," Royce said slowly. He took a drink.

A smile flicked over her mouth and she shook it off. Royce looked at her. Although she smiled infrequently, it was very becoming when she did. In the half-light of the bedroom the pockmarks on her face looked two-dimensional, like freckles. Her dark shoulder peeked out of the mantle of her long hair like a rock in a black river. The crease where her belly met her thigh reminded him of the rounded hills of California. The toes clustered beneath her behind looked like water-rounded pebbles at the base of a smooth stone.

He drank again. He could get used to this geology. To hell with Eddie.

He reached to touch her. She slipped off the bed and left the room.

Royce lay back against the wall and sipped the whiskey. She'd get used to it. She had to. A woman can't make it without help. It's a man's world out there, and that wasn't just his opinion. Lots of people said so. He'd help Colleen, though. He'd be her man. She'd be fine with him. He could set up a little practice in some border town some-where, way out beyond Del Rio maybe, in Big Bend country. They could live up in the mountains, keep a little ranch with some brood stock on it. Sell a few horses, deliver a few babies, maintain a couple of sensible morphine habits.

He heard her walking over the empty potato-chip bags in the other room.

Funny how that stuff makes you itch. And scratching doesn't do you any good. He idly scratched the length of his forearm against the label of the whiskey bottle. His hands had stopped shaking, and he was sweating normally, like any man in summer in Texas. How quick-ly the system adapts to outrage. Murder and dope. Franklin Royce was a new man. He noticed the whiskey took the edge off his desire for the morphine but didn't really quench it. No wonder addicts wandered between junk addiction and alcohol addiction and back.

Well, that wouldn't be a problem for him and Colleen. Pharmaceutical morphine is not very expensive when you have a license to buy it. The trick is not to get too strung out, not to get to where you can't maintain a semblance of normal life. Keep on eating, drinking, working and keeping the dosage light. Temperance in all things. That's the key.

He heard the toilet flush in the far end of the apartment.

Plumbing, he thought. Like any woman, she'll be wanting plumbing. So we can't get too far up in the mountains. Trip to El Paso once in a while; get a pair of fancy boots. Would she be good with the horses? Women usually are, if they get on with them at all. But first what we have to do is figure out how to get rid of Past Eddie, and we're free to go. Poor old Past Eddie. He turned and looked at the corpse, to his right across the bed. The corpse stared back at the bottle. Poor old Past Eddie, my ass. Got just what he deserved. Shooting women in the face. Framing his best friend. Well, Eddie, how do you like the swift retribution, huh? A real eye-opener, eh?

Just then Colleen Valdez came back into the bedroom. She was wearing the saffron taffeta housecoat he'd first met her in, unsecured in front, and she was carrying Eddie's guitar. Without a word to Royce, she went to the other side of the bed and placed the guitar in the dead man's lap and rested the peghead over his shoulder against the wall. She stepped back and regarded the effect of this for a moment, giving Royce a chance once again to admire her charms. Never would he tire of looking at her. After a moment Colleen stepped forward to make an adjustment. She wrapped Eddie's blue checked arm over the guitar. The strings twanged and damped as she stepped back again.

"He always loved his guitar," she said, apparently satisfied with the mordant tableau. "He once told me he wanted to be buried with it. In case they had taverns in hell, he said, he could always play for drinks. Now." She turned to the window and turned back, holding up a syringe in each hand. She looked at Royce. "This has all been a great strain on me. May I trouble you for an injection, Doctor?"

Royce brightened, like a naughty little boy once again back in the good graces of his mother. He set the bottle on the floor next to the bed and held out his hand for the tools of his trade. Colleen stepped over Eddie's inert legs onto the bed, and stood over Royce.

"Do both of us, Royce," she said, looking down at him from the high shadows of her hair. In the orange and black she looked like a storm sunset. Then she dropped the housecoat. "Afterwards, I'll do both of us," she whispered.

He smiled up at her. "I'd be happy to oblige, and to be obliged, ma'am."

She knelt beside him and handed him a syringe. He took her left arm. "Alcohol," he said.

"Fuck the alcohol," she said huskily, and ran her free hand along his leg.

"Don't fuck the alcohol; fuck the alcoholic," Royce chided her. He picked up the bottle, took a slug of whiskey into his mouth and held it there. Then he kissed and licked the inside of her elbow. She giggled. "That'll clean it off," he said with gallant authority. He swabbed her arm with the whiskey and tied it off. He carefully chose a spot with the thin, short diabetic needle and hit her cleanly among the small red dots already on her arm. She sighed and sat back on her heels. She removed the tubing herself as he pressed the plunger home and withdrew the point. Royce dropped the spent hypodermic to the floor and picked up the whiskey bottle. He drank, then inverted the bottle on his thumb. She licked her finger and dabbed at the spot of blood on her arm.

"God, you're good at that, Royce," she said breathily. "It's the one aspect of the whole tour I've never really liked, shooting myself up. But you make it... easy...."

"Force of habit," he explained sheepishly, as he dabbed whiskey on the inside of his forearm over a prominent vein. "Like hygiene."

"Hi, Gene." She stroked him dreamily. "I don't mind a habit or two," she said, as she lovingly tied an overhand knot in the surgical tubing, around his arm below the bicep. "It's people messing with my life I don't like."

He held the syringe upside down and tapped it to get the air to the tip of the needle. Then he gently depressed the plunger until a droplet appeared at its tip. "That's all over now, baby." He winced as he punctured his skin and the wall of the vein and slid the needle into his forearm. It always felt like a train entering a tunnel to him. "I was thinking," he said, as a thin red feather of his blood appeared in the syringe, "once we get rid of Eddie there'll be no reason to stick around here.... Hey, you know?" He looked up at her. She was watching the needle at his arm. "I was wondering."

"About what?" she said softly, releasing the knot.

"Oh," Royce said, as he looked down again at his work and began to depress the plunger. "How come Eddie never snake-bit you, like he did Bobby and me and I guess everybody else he wanted to push around?" The plunger eased down.

"Maybe he thought I'd been snake-bit enough," she said thoughtfully. She touched two fingertips to the twin burns on Royce's neck.

He slipped the needle from his arm and smiled up at her. "Oh?" he said lazily. The angle of her face, the smooth oval of black hair framing it, the look her skin had of pitted marble, once again it all struck him as elements of a Pieta, a gentle fond mother leaning over the squirming marble child in her lap. But he couldn't summon the energy to tell her.

She watched her hand as she drew it gently over his shoulder, along his ribs, down his thigh, and said, "You killed the wrong guy, Royce." She held his sex and raised her eyes to his. Royce's face became genuinely puzzled. By now she was pretty stoned herself, a languid morphine girl, and she wet her lips once, twice. "I called Thurman the other day, while I was out for groceries." She nodded. The look on Royce's face had turned to genuine bewilderment, and his breath had gone shallow and noisy. "You don't have enough time to understand it all, Royce," she said. "But you should know that the store robbery went exactly as I told you it did, except for one detail."

"No," Royce protested, as his vision blurred into the colors of her nipples.

"That's right," she said, leaning forward. "Eddie didn't kill that woman clerk." She covered his mouth with hers. Her pitted skin became an enlarged lunar surface as her lips met his lips, and she kissed him. "I did," she whispered into his mouth before her tongue entered it.

The truth of his error, the tremendous finality of his mistake and this penultimate repercussion advanced through his mind like a seething, enormous wave. He felt her tongue pass thickly between his lips, swell and stick to the walls of his mouth, filling it completely, dessicating it, only to dissolve in the absorbed fluids there, as if the paradox were that he secreted corrosive acids upon her tender flesh, not the other way around. Then the wave broke with a crash and Royce died.

Colleen Valdez sat back on her heels. Royce's open eyes saw nothing.

She explained things to him anyway.

"Thurman was real good to Bobby Mink, you know; he really loved that Bobby," she continued, sighing as if she were very tired. "He told me all about how you were the prison doctor, and about how you helped put Bobby down.... He said..."

The morphine was becoming too much for her. Had Royce not been dead, he might have modestly explained to her how he'd done what he could for Bobby Mencken at the end. As he was silent, she pulled herself to the head of the bed and slouched against the wall, much like her two companions flanking her. She clutched fitfully for a moment at the sheets with her fingers, but everybody was on top of them and she soon gave up. "Damn," she whispered, in a sing-song, little girl voice. "Damn, damn, damn." Then she sighed. "Bobby, Bobby, Bobby. He wouldn't let me take my medicine for killing that old woman, and I never had a chance to talk him out of it. I never saw him but once again after they arrested him, except in the newspapers and on TV. Eddie kept telling me it wouldn't do any good to go telling the police my story, that they'd never believe a woman had done what they had Bobby for...."

"Thurman said you got the whole file on Bobby, Royce, and said my name was on it from when I visited Bobby that one time and he told me to never come back because it was too hard on him to see me, and not be able to… to do anything but look and remember. He said seeing me was the hardest thing he'd had to do since he got to prison, and to please don't make him go through it again…. Just… Just go with Eddie and do the best we could, and, remember… he loved us…."

Though her eyes were closed now, hot tears fell out of them as if out of a permanent condition, as if a lifetime of this helpless seepage had scalded the surface of her face to its present state of irreparable corrosion.

But soon she fell asleep as she was, for the morphine was good, and she felt secure, secure in the knowledge that another syringe full of morphine was just within reach, just on the other side of Eddie, behind the curtain on the window-sill, right where Royce had left it. So she could have another shot as soon as she woke up….

The police found them there just like that, the three of them in bed together, the narcotized girl between two naked corpses, about half an hour later.

Fast Eddie hadn't been so fast after all.